Raja Balushahi and Rani Rasmalai in Mithaspur

& Other Adventures

Raja Balushahi and Rani Rasmalai in Mithaspur
& Other Adventures

Prashant Pinge

Illustrated by
Priya Kuriyan

HarperCollins*Children's Books*

First published in India in 2018 by HarperCollins Children's Books
An imprint of HarperCollins *Publishers*

HarperCollins Publishers India, Cyber City, Building 10-A, Gurugram,
Haryana-122002, India
www.harpercollins.co.in

2 4 6 8 10 9 7 5 3 1

P-ISBN: 978-93-5302-300-3

Typeset by Ateendriya
in Georgia, 10.5 pt and Carnivalee Freakshow, 30 pt

Printed and bound at
MicroPrints India, New Delhi

MIX
Paper
FSC FSC® C218906

This product is made of FSC®-certified and other controlled material.

HarperCollins Publishers, Macken House, 39/40 Mayor Street
Upper, Dublin 1, D01 C9W8, Ireland

CONTENTS

THE MAGIC LADDOO

'What if all the laddoos aren't recovered?' gulped Raja Balushahi, the King of Mithaspur, glancing fearfully at his queen, Rani Rasmalai. He pried out a tutti frutti from his crown and pushed it absentmindedly into his mouth. 'If someone from Manav Lok gets their hands on even one, I shall be in so much trouble with the Mahanagri Parishad. Even the thought of it is making my sides crumble.'

It had been almost two days since Mawali—a slippery, beady-eyed kachori with a spoiled mawa filling—had stolen a jar of magic laddoos from the royal sweet factory and snuck into Manav Lok. If a single laddoo fell into the hands of a child, they would be able to enter Chamatkar Nagri – something that was strictly forbidden.

'Don't worry, Balu darling,' said Rani Rasmalai in her soft, creamy voice, gently stroking the bright orange kesar strands of his hair. 'Our kachoris will find all the laddoos before you know it. And I think you look really cute when your cheeks flake.'

Raja Balushahi squeezed his queen's face lovingly – some of the sugar syrup dripped down. 'You always know just the right thing to say, my dear,' he smiled. But the very next moment, his thick brown coating was coming apart.

'What if they don't? How can I explain this mess to the Mahanagri Parishad?'

The king was about to have a breakdown when a patter of feet rang through the palace. It was a group of roly-poly kachoris balancing a large glass jar on their shoulders. 'We've found the magic laddoos, Maharaj,' they chimed in chorus. 'And Mawali has been locked inside our deepest, darkest dungeon.'

Raja Balushahi clapped and twirled around in joy. 'You shall all be rewarded with your favourite badam halwa. And Mawali shall be sent to Thappad Pradesh.'

But he had barely raised his goblet of sweet mango lassi when a trembling kachori stumbled into the royal chamber. 'Big ... big ... problem, Maharaj,' he panted, some of his sweet mawa spilling out.

'Are we falling short of rose syrup again?' sighed the king, rolling his raisin eyes. 'Or is it the ground cashews this time?'

'Worse, Maharaj,' stammered the kachori. 'Shwetvardhan, the senior elder, has just sent a message. Krooradasa has escaped.'

'What?' sputtered the king, knocking over the goblet and sending the mango lassi flying all over.

The queen looked worried. 'It was you who banished him into the Bhool Bhulaiya, wasn't it?'

'Two hundred years ago, my queen. And now, he'll be seeking revenge.'

Before either of them could speak, the kachori squeaked apologetically. 'Maharaj, Krooradasa has also stolen the Pitambari wand.'

Raja Balushahi almost had his stuffing knocked out. 'Not the Pitambari wand,' he wailed. 'It's the most powerful wand ever made. Even if I was younger and stronger, I wouldn't be able to stop him now.'

Meanwhile, in Manav Lok ...

'Not again,' groaned Arjun, as the fan gave a gasp. He followed the rotating blades as they slowed down and cranked to a halt. 'That's the third time today.'

Anindita, his nine-year-old sister, promptly brought up the magazine lying by her side and began to fan herself. She was busy reading stories from the Panchatantra.

Arjun plopped down on the bed. 'I'm bored, Anu,' he mumbled, pulling a pillow over his head. He peeped out from below a few moments later. 'Didn't you hear me? I'm bored.'

'It's only been a couple of days since we got here,' sighed Anindita, shaking her head at him. 'We have another month to go.'

The siblings were spending their summer vacation in the village with their grandparents. But things weren't going exactly as planned. Arjun ran his fingers through his dark brown hair and stared at the ceiling. His sister was right. How would he survive in this place for that long?

'Why don't we go for a walk?' Anindita said, keeping her book aside. 'I really feel like eating something sweet after that spicy coconut curry Dadi made.'

Arjun was about to protest but ended up nodding reluctantly. There really wasn't much else to do anyway. He had finished reading all his science books. He was tired of playing video games on his phone. And with the power outage, it only made sense to step out instead of getting baked inside the house.

'Isn't it a lovely day?' remarked Anindita, spreading her arms to the clear blue skies as the cool breeze from the surrounding mountains played with her dark brown curls.

Arjun simply flapped his lips in reply. Was there anything else he could do? He hung his head and stepped onto the porch with a sigh.

The two walked down the broken path that wound its way into the small market. The shop they were looking for was hidden between an old cycle repair joint and a dimly lit grocery. Surprisingly, it was quite cosy, with a long glass counter packed with neatly arranged rows of brightly coloured sweets. Anindita took a deep breath, marvelling at the delicious fragrance that wafted through the air. After almost five minutes of going back and forth, Arjun finally settled on a piece of rose barfi. Anindita wanted to go for a delicious laddoo.

She was about to point to it when one particular laddoo lodged in the corner of the tray caught her eye. It was the only one that had a sprinkling of delicate

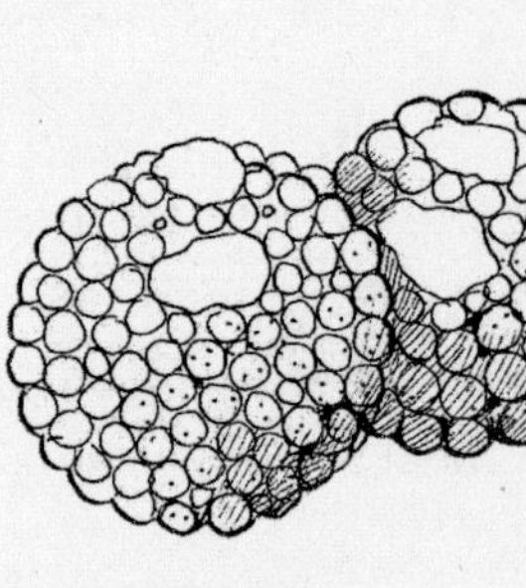

silver foil on its freckled golden-yellow surface. 'I'll have that one,' she piped, pushing her tiny finger against the glass. She swivelled on her toes, eyes shining. 'Why don't we take these to the woods?'

'I suppose,' shrugged Arjun, paying for the sweets.

'Doesn't mine look magical?'

'Don't be silly, Anu. It's just a laddoo.'

But he couldn't have been more wrong. For Raja Balushahi's kachoris had managed to recover all the laddoos but one.

The lush green woods stretched from the back of the house, where they disappeared into the foothills of the mountains. Arjun found a quiet spot in a small clearing. A thin layer of mist surrounded them.

Anindita brought out the laddoo from the bag. 'Why don't we share it?' she said, peeling out the soft delicacy. She was about to throw the paper cup when her eyes fell on something. 'Look, Arjun, there's something written inside.'

'I'm sure it's nothing,' said Arjun, breaking the laddoo in half.

Anindita brushed away the crumbs and peered closely. She caught a glint across the wrapper as silver text appeared. 'It's some kind of a poem. Let me read it out.'

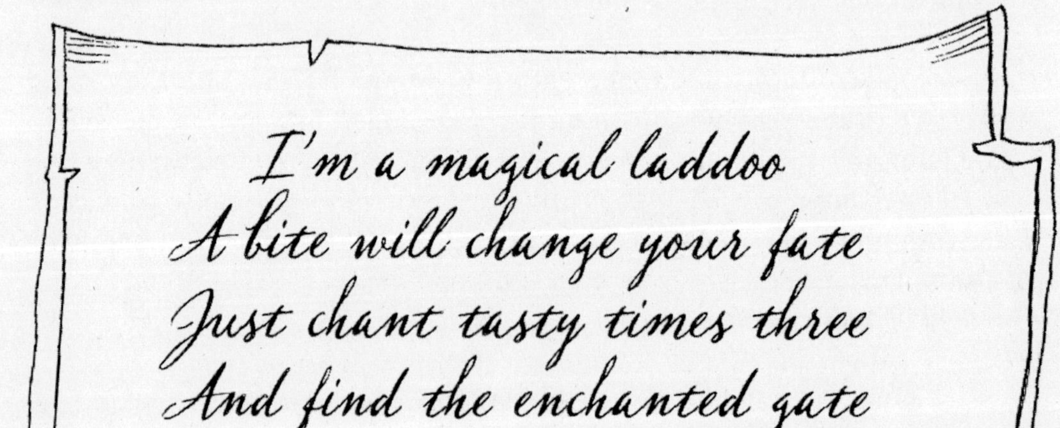

'Really,' said Arjun, rolling his eyes. 'So, if I take a bite of this laddoo and say "tasty" thrice, I will see a magical gate? This has to be the weirdest gimmick I've ever come across.'

'Why don't we try?' said Anindita excitedly. 'You never know.'

'Okay,' smiled Arjun, joining in the fun. He knew his sister was just teasing.

So they both took a bite out of their laddoo halves and chanted 'tasty' three times. Anindita looked around, half-expecting a door to show up. But the stillness remained undisturbed. Arjun had a wry smile on his face and an eyebrow cocked at his sister. He was about to make a mean comment when he noticed the disappointed look on her face. 'Come on, Anu,' he said, putting an arm around her. 'You didn't really expect a gate to appear, did you?'

Anindita blinked her eyes, before slipping the paper cup inside her pocket. 'Let's just go back,' she said in a glum voice.

But they had hardly taken a few steps when Arjun abruptly stopped in his tracks. Something wasn't quite right. He pinched the tip of his nose as he scanned the surroundings. There were trees all around. And then, as the mist began to fade away, he saw it.

Anindita had been so lost in her thoughts that it took her a few minutes to realize her brother wasn't by her side. 'Arjun?' she said, turning around. 'What's the matter?'

Arjun, who had fallen behind, simply looked at her with his mouth wide open, pointing to his right with a trembling finger. When Anindita turned in that direction, she could feel her heart pounding against her ribcage. The mist had cleared to reveal a door, floating in between the trees.

'It worked,' whispered Anindita, clasping her hands together.

'It ... it can't be,' gulped Arjun, goggling at the sight. 'There has to be a logical explanation. Perhaps we're dreaming. Or it's just an illusion.'

But it wasn't. It was a door all right, made of solid mahogany and almost twice his height. Anindita ran over and moved her fingers along the surface, feeling the intricately carved designs, until they reached the polished brass knob.

'There's nothing here,' said Arjun, knocking from behind. He popped his head from the side. 'I don't understand. It's just standing here.'

'Should we open it?' asked Anindita, curling her fingers around the knob.

Arjun bit the end of his lips. What in the world was a door doing in the middle of nowhere? And where did it lead to? Perhaps it was better to leave some questions unanswered. But he was gripped by an intense curiosity.

Anindita turned the knob with both hands. The door creaked open slowly, sending a cloud of dust into the air – a sign that it hadn't been opened in a very long time. Only, it wasn't dust but fine cinnamon powder. The two waited anxiously as it slowly settled.

The door had opened into a beautiful garden that could only be described as magical. It was bathed in the golden glow that was bursting out of the azure skies. The wind whispered through the leafy canopies of several lopsided trees that lined the garden. A cobbled path ran through the gentle rolling mounds that were covered with weirdly shaped plants. The water from artistically sculpted fountains flowed in tune to the soothing music that filled the air. And at the far end stood a magnificent castle, its towers disappearing into the pink clouds above. It was a completely mesmerizing sight.

'Jalebis are growing on this plant,' shrieked Anindita, breaking a piece of the sticky, glazed orange sweet. She popped it in her mouth and sighed contentedly. 'It's delicious.'

Arjun was busy trying to reach some strangely familiar dark red fruits on a tree nearby. When he finally managed to pluck one, he was delighted to find that it was a gulab jamun! 'This is unbelievable,' he mumbled, happily chomping the fried milk ball dipped in honey.

'And look at this patch,' laughed Anindita. She had run over to one of the mounds. 'The flower petals are pieces of kaju katli. And there's a small rasgulla inside each!'

While Anindita marvelled at the view, Arjun made his way to the fountain, only to discover—much to his delight—that it was dispensing chilled nimbu pani. He was about to scoop up a handful when chaos broke out in the garden, causing him to almost topple over.

'Children from Manav Lok!' 'How did they come here?' 'Call the guards.' The place was filled with confused and frightened shrieks.

Turns out that Arjun and Anindita had ended up in Raja Balushahi's garden. And while they were exploring the garden, Rani Rasmalai and her malai maids also happened to be taking a round.

Both Arjun and Anindita were stunned to see the delicate-looking creamy white queen with beautiful pistachio eyes and slender limbs surrounded by the waifish malai maids, all of whom were now running helter-skelter.

'We're ... we're really sorry,' said an alarmed Anindita. 'We found this door. And it opened into this place.'

'What's going on here?' thundered a loud voice from a pergola some distance away. Raja Balushahi had been deep in concentration under the dome made of peanut chikki, trying hard to come up with spells to counter Krooradasa, when the disturbance had occurred.

Rani Rasmalai and her maids watched the kesar strands on the king's head bobbing above the hedge as he walked over.

'Children from Manav Lok,' groaned Raja Balushahi in utter despair. But he was also secretly relieved as it could well have been the evil jadugar. 'Why does all this have to happen right now? Why can't these problems come one by one?'

Rani Rasmalai looked anxiously at his deepening brown cheeks. 'Balu, darling, the children would have been a problem under normal circumstances. But don't we have bigger issues to tackle right now? Our focus should be on defeating Krooradasa.'

'Who is this Krooradasa?' asked Anindita, unable to stop herself.

'He's a wicked jadugar,' replied the queen. And she told them about Krooradasa's escape and how he was coming after Raja Balushahi for revenge.

'Perhaps we can help you. My brother is really smart.'

Arjun stumbled back a few paces as everyone's eyes turned towards him. He was about to point out that no matter how highly his sister regarded his intelligence, he was only 11. But when he saw how anxious everyone looked, he slowly nodded and said, 'I ... I'll do my best.'

'It's settled then,' said a relieved Raja Balushahi. 'Let's head to the palace.'

'So where exactly are we?' asked Arjun, licking a conical piece of strawberry kulfi at the end of a stick.

Raja Balushahi, who had been mulling over the spells he could use, snapped out of his thoughts. 'This is Mithaspur,' he replied. 'It's a part of Chamatkar Nagri.'

'I would have pinched myself, but I've already done that so many times. It's still hard to believe we're actually here.'

'So can you really help me?' asked Raja Balushahi, fiddling with his hair.

'Well,' said Arjun, scratching his chin, 'if this Pitambari wand is as powerful as you say it is ...'

'... yes, yes, it's very powerful ...'

'... then mere magic may not be the best way to go.'

'What do you mean?'

'I think the way out of this situation would be to outwit him.'

Raja Balushahi sat up with a start. Was it really possible? Could they actually outsmart the jadugar? It was certainly an idea worth considering. After all, his spells didn't stand a chance against the power of the Pitambari wand.

'Now let's see,' said Arjun, emptying the contents of his pockets. Out came a small torch he was carrying in case there was a power outage; a rose barfi, which now seemed quite ordinary; and some loose change. 'By the way, when is this Krooradasa expected?'

'I would say after dark, since he's a jadugar of the night.'

Arjun tapped his fingers on the table for a few moments. 'I may just have a plan,' he said, slowly picking up the torch.

'I told you Arjun was clever,' said Anindita, beaming at her brother with pride.

'I want you to find a spell that is simple and works quickly. We won't have much time. You have to use it the moment I shout 'now'. Leave the rest to me.'

'What is that?' asked Rani Rasmalai, pointing at the torch.

'It's a simple gadget that I hope will help us defeat Krooradasa. Anindita, I will need your help. I will also need a few other things.'

While Arjun explained his plan to Anindita and the queen, Raja Balushahi got busy searching for a spell. He finally found one that could be used to turn someone into a piece of dry toast.

The skies above Mithaspur had taken on a depressing grey hue, with dark clouds casting a grim shadow on the palace grounds. The sweet fragrance had disappeared, replaced by the stench of impending doom. The music had died long since, and all that could be heard was the monotonous buzzing of flies. The once beautiful garden seemed to be under a curse that had snatched its soul, leaving a trail of misery in its wake. And just when one thought that things couldn't get any worse, a coarse voice—like a nail being dragged across a chalkboard—pierced the putrid air.

'Balushahi, you scoundrel, show your miserable face so that I can smash it into a thousand crumbs.'

It was Krooradasa, seething with fury. Suddenly, lightning flashes struck the mound on which he stood, revealing the evil jadugar. He was tall and thin; dirty robes hung loosely around his shrivelled body that seemed to be giving off black fumes. His face was shrouded in the shadow of his limp hat, but even the darkness could not mask his rabid yellow eyes that shone from the bony sockets underneath. And for a brief moment, as the lightning reduced the tree stump by his side to ashes, you could see a long, shiny wand clutched between his trembling fingers.

'You puny fellow,' shouted the jadugar, hurling a blaze of ochre into the skies, 'did you think I would forgive you? Two hundred years. That's how long I have spent in the Bhool Bhulaiyya. And I spent every single moment planning my revenge.'

Raja Balushahi stepped out of the pergola, as confidently as he could, with his wand drawn. 'You're going to have a few hundred years more to do your thinking, because I'm going to send you back.'

'How dare you mock me!' shouted Krooradasa, raising the Pitambari wand. Just then, in the fleeting glow of the lightning, he noticed Arjun and Anindita on two mounds alongside. The jadugar smirked. 'Children? Are you so weak that you bring children into battle?'

'Are you afraid?' taunted Raja Balushahi, struggling to hold his voice steady.

Krooradasa flew into a rage. 'I will turn you all into spiders and dance upon you till you become pulp. I shall ... wait ... what is that?'

But Anindita wasn't going to wait. She shone the torch directly into his face. The jadugar stumbled back in shock as the powerful glare hit his eyes, blinding him temporarily. Arjun was waiting for this. He immediately launched pieces of hard chikki at him like tiny missiles. The second one caught Krooradasa sharply on the hand. A scream of agony rose from his throat, almost drowning the claps of thunder.

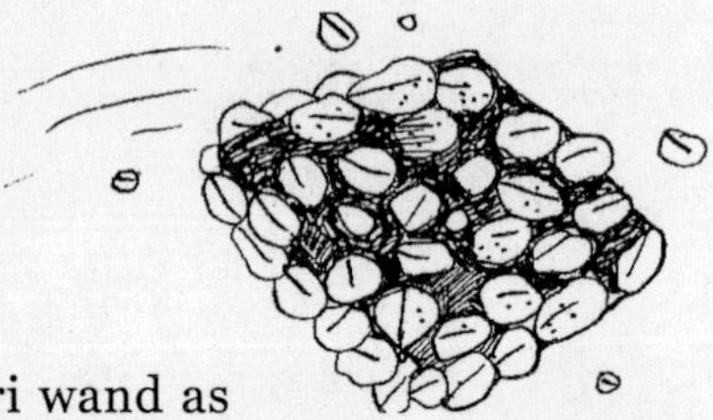

'Now,' shouted Arjun, as Raja Balushahi hurled a spell at his nemesis.

Alas, the jadugar had not dropped the Pitambari wand as expected. Instead, it had cast a protective shield around him, and Raja Balushahi's spell fizzled out. 'You will all pay for this,' hissed Krooradasa, pointing the wand at his sworn enemy. The tip began to glow, gently at first and then like red hot embers, until it shot out a bolt of lightning at the King of Mithaspur.

Raja Balushahi barely managed to roll out of the way, leaving a deep shimmering tear at the place where he had stood moments before. The jadugar, frustrated at missing his target, strode ahead, ready to hurl another bolt at the fallen king. Blinded by rage, he did not see the thin strings that Arjun had criss-crossed along the garden floor. The very next moment, his foot caught in the strings and he tipped forward. Krooradasa clutched the wand tightly but could not maintain his balance. And unfortunately for him, it struck the ground first, shattering into three pieces.

'Now!' Arjun's voice echoed in the quiet of the night once again.

Raja Balushahi hurled the spell at the fallen jadugar. The hat and robes fell limply to the ground. Moments later, they were all staring at a harmless piece of toast. They had actually succeeded in defeating the mighty Krooradasa. But it had been a very close call.

'Mithaspur owes you a debt of gratitude,' said Raja Balushahi, hugging them both. 'I shudder to think what would have happened had you not found that laddoo. You shall forever be welcome in Chamatkar Nagri.'

'It's time for a feast,' Rani Rasmalai's voice floated in from the terrace.

And what a feast it was! Arjun and Anindita ate so much they could hardly move. Before long, it was time to leave. A white mist wafted out of Raja Balushahi's wand and wrapped itself gently around the children. They soon drifted off to sleep.

'Arjun, I had the strangest dream,' said Anindita, sitting up and stretching her arms. 'We had both travelled to ...'

'It wasn't a dream,' said Arjun, pulling out some kaju-katli petals from his pocket. 'Besides, we both couldn't have had the same dream.'

Anindita felt the soft grass under her palms. 'It was real,' she whispered. 'It all actually happened. What an adventure!'

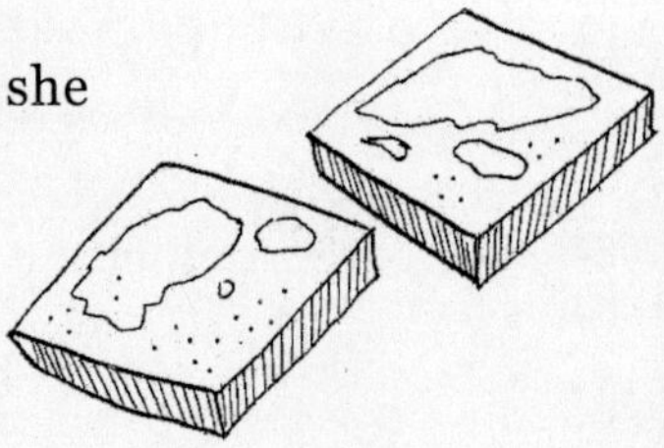

'It was, but I suppose we should head back. And not a word to anyone.'

'I wonder if we will ever visit Chamatkar Nagri again.'

Little did she know that this was just the beginning of many more magical adventures to come.

Paan Ki Begum

The market square of Jaduprastha, the capital of Chamatkar Nagri, was abuzz with nervous chatter. A grave calamity had befallen Tashkot, the land of cards.

'Isn't it terrible?' exclaimed the pari, picking up a beautiful pink shawl made of dried bougainvillea petals. 'But who would kidnap Paan Ki Begum? She's so kind and generous.'

The stumpy yaksha behind the counter leaned forward. 'I've heard it's none other than Dushtasura.'

The pari sucked in her breath sharply. 'The asura warlord from Paschimi Ilaka? What will happen now?'

'He'll make demands, what else?' said a kinnari, who had wandered by. She reached for a basket woven with sparkling moonbeams. 'He's such an evil fellow. How much for this?'

'Only two gold mudras,' the yaksha replied. He pulled out a few lotus leaves to pack it after receiving a nod. 'I hope they get her back safely.'

Meanwhile, the Mahanagri Parishad was in an emergency meeting at Suvarna Minar, the most powerful place of magic in Chamatkar Nagri.

'How did this tragedy happen?' asked Pavitranandan, an elder in the Mahanagri Parishad.

'It was a case of sheer misfortune,' replied Bhadradharma, the elder of the western region. 'The four badshahs and begums of Tashkot were vacationing along the border, near Lobhvan. It's forbidden to wander inside the forest since Paschimi Ilaka lies on the other side. Paan Ki Begum, however, did not heed the warning and strayed inside. Unfortunately, Dushtasura also happened to be prowling around and, finding her wandering alone, captured her. He now has her imprisoned in Veeran Gadh.'

The crystal ball at the centre of the round table suddenly became misty and started to glow. On it appeared a face with dark brown hair flowing under a magnificent bejewelled red crown. It was a distraught Paan Ka Badshah.

'Dushtasura has sent across his demands,' he said. 'He wants all the four badshahs to declare Tashkot to be a part of Paschimi Ilaka. This means we shall have to hand over the four royal sceptres to him within the next 24 hours. If we fail to do so, he has threatened to turn my begum into a black beetle.'

'Is there anything we can do?' asked Bhadradharma.

'It would be foolish to attack Paschimi Ilaka, since that scoundrel is holding my begum captive. Although the other badshahs have agreed to give up their thrones, it wouldn't be fair to them or to the people of Tashkot. But I'm so lost without my beloved begum.'

'Should we send word to Shwetvardhan?' asked Gyandarshan, a young elder. 'His wisdom will be invaluable at this dreadful time.'

Bhadradharma shook his head slowly. 'Shwetvardhan must not be disturbed under any circumstances today,' he sighed. 'He's on the southern edge of Chamatkar Nagri, conducting some very delicate negotiations with the mythical monsters.'

'I suppose it's up to us then to find a solution,' said Pavitranandan, his brow deeply furrowed. 'This situation can escalate quickly if we don't nip it in the bud.'

Meanwhile, in Manav Lok ...

Arjun stared at the bright orange sun, whose magnificent colours were bleeding into the dense clouds as it made its final descent. But the beauty of the scene was lost upon its beholder. The only thing it reminded him of was the magic laddoo that had earlier taken them to Chamatkar Nagri.

'Should we try the sweet shop again?' asked Anindita, her voice brimming with hope.

Arjun clutched his stomach and turned away. 'No more laddoos, please. I must have eaten more than 10 in the past two days.'

The two had spent hours in the woods, searching for the enchanted door, but it was nowhere to be found. They had then headed back to the shop in the hope of unearthing another magic laddoo. But it had all been for nothing.

'So what should we do now?' asked Anindita in a low voice, pulling at a loose thread in the bedsheet.

Arjun was about to draw the curtains when his eyes fell upon a deck of cards. 'We could play cards.' He shrugged, tossing the deck to her. 'How about a game of Challenge?'

'I suppose.'

'You can deal first.'

Anindita removed the cards and began to shuffle them. Just then, a card popped out and fell upon the bed. 'That's strange,' she said, picking it up. 'Have a look at this card, Arjun. Is it my imagination or is the queen of hearts fading right before my eyes?'

'She ... she's disappearing,' gulped Arjun, scrunching his nose. He pulled the card closer. 'Yes, she's definitely getting lighter. What's happening?'

Just then, there was a tapping sound. When the children turned, they were surprised to see a pari on the window sill. Anindita could hardly contain her excitement as Arjun raised the glass pane.

'I'm Leela,' said the pari, fluttering inside and landing softly upon a pillow. 'If you may please, we need your help urgently in Chamatkar Nagri.'

'Has it got anything to do with the queen of hearts?' asked Anindita.

'It does. But there isn't any time to explain. We must reach Tashkot right away. Bhadradharma, the respected elder, will explain everything once we get there.'

'But how do we get there? The door to Chamatkar Nagri has disappeared!'

'Of course, it has,' said Leela matter-of-factly. 'It's gone to visit some friends.'

Arjun and Anindita stared at each other. A door with friends! What next?

'But don't worry. I can take you there in no time.' And with that, the dainty pari picked up the deck of cards and started to chant.

Shuffle the cards with care
Make sure you have a full hand
Throw them up in the air
Deal your way into card land

Leela flung the cards above their heads. But instead of falling down, they remained frozen in the air. And then, slowly, the cards started to flap, before beginning to swirl around—gently at first, and then with the ferocity of a hurricane—until everything became blurry. Seconds later, the cards fell down in a swoop to reveal Tashkot.

Arjun and Anindita were taken aback at the spectacle that unfolded before their eyes. The entire place was made of cards – from all the roads that criss-crossed the land to the trees at each corner, from the quaint little cars moving by to the houses that were neatly arranged in rows. And everywhere they looked, they were greeted with motifs of the four suits—spades, hearts, diamonds and clubs—arranged in kaleidoscopic patterns of red and black. But the most amazing part was the residents of Tashkot, each of whom was a playing card, only larger, with a head on top and skinny arms and legs sticking out from the side and bottom. Unfortunately, though, there wasn't any time to explore.

Bhadradharma and the four badshahs of Tashkot were waiting for the children inside the Patta Mahal, a spectacular palace made entirely of playing cards. Their faces brightened up a little at the sight of Arjun and Anindita.

'Welcome to Tashkot,' said Bhadradharma, stepping forward. He had a kind face with gentle eyes and sharp, slender features. A long, grey beard ran down his simple white robes.

Anindita stepped behind Arjun shyly.

'We find ourselves in a very grave situation. Dushtasura has kidnapped Paan Ki Begum.'

'No wonder she's disappearing from the card,' said Arjun.

'Exactly,' replied the elder. 'Earlier today, Raja Balushahi informed me about your heroics. We were hoping you could help us as well.'

Arjun could feel his throat go dry. Dushtasura did not sound like a pleasant character. He somehow managed a nod. 'Perhaps you can tell me everything that has happened so far.'

Paan Ka Badshah narrated the events that had led to the kidnapping and the subsequent demands put forth by the asura warlord.

'You mentioned Paschimi Ilaka? What exactly is this?'

'Paschimi Ilaka lies to the west of Chamatkar Nagri,' replied Bhadradharma, smoothing his robes. 'Many thousand years ago, both were part of one great land, Punyabhoomi. But a group of evil jadugars and asuras tried to overthrow the Mahanagri Parishad. After a fierce battle that raged for 40 days and 40 nights, a peace treaty was forged, and the land was divided into two parts.'

'And can you tell me something about this Dushtasura?'

'While things have largely remained peaceful between our lands, there are still some in Paschimi Ilaka who want to control Chamatkar Nagri as it's a source of very powerful magic. Dushtasura is one of those rogue asura warlords. He stays in Veeran Gadh, just across the border beyond Lobhvan, the forest of temptations.'

'So what options do we have?'

Huqum Ka Badshah spoke up. 'The first is to surrender the four royal sceptres to Dushtasura. However, once he takes over Tashkot, he will be emboldened to attack the other lands in Chamatkar Nagri. The second option is to not give in to his demands, but he has threatened to turn Paan Ki Begum into a black beetle. So we obviously cannot tread down that path.'

'We most certainly cannot,' said Paan Ka Badshah with a shudder.

'A third option, however, does exist,' said Bhadradharma in a grave tone. 'We must rescue Paan Ki Begum from the clutches of Dushtasura. And that is where you come in.'

'But what can I do against an asura? I don't know any magic.'

'And yet you managed to overcome Krooradasa.'

'We had help from Raja Balushahi. Besides, won't it just be easier for you to send someone from Chamatkar Nagri to save the queen?'

Bhadradharma pressed the bridge of his nose. 'It's not as simple as that,' he sighed. 'If we send someone from here and they get caught, Dushtasura will surely turn Paan Ki Begum into a beetle. It can also give the rogues in Paschimi Ilaka an excuse to call for an attack on Chamatkar Nagri. But we may just have a chance with a human child.'

Arjun exhaled slowly. How could he face an asura warlord alone? Would he also be turned into some insect? He wiped the beads of perspiration from his brow. 'I ... I don't know.'

'Please say yes,' pleaded Paan Ka Badshah, clasping his hands. 'Every moment away from my beloved begum feels like an eternity.'

'There is one more problem,' added Bhadradharma sombrely. 'If Tashkot is lost, all the pictures on the cards in Manav Lok will disappear.'

Arjun closed his eyes and let his head fall forward. 'Fine,' he nodded, squaring his jaw. 'I'm ready.'

Paan Ka Badshah gave him a tight hug. 'Thank you so much.'

'Don't worry, we shan't be sending you into Paschimi Ilaka unprepared,' said Bodhidharma. 'You shall take the Gayabana, also known as the cloak of invisibility.'

Chidee Ka Badshah walked towards Arjun, his arms outstretched. He then threw them around Arjun's back.

'You ... you've disappeared from below your neck,' gasped Anindita, staring at his floating head. She slowly jabbed her finger at him and got the soft part of his arm.

Arjun could feel his body, but when he looked down, he found himself staring at the mosaic on the floor. 'This is so cool,' he said, sliding the cloak off gently. 'Is there anything else?'

'As a matter of fact, there is,' said Bodhidharma, bringing out a small glass bottle filled with a dense, green substance. 'This is a magical ointment that can open any door. Use it wisely.'

'The plan is very simple,' said Huqum Ka Badshah. 'You enter Paschimi Ilaka wearing the cloak of invisibility and locate Paan Ki Begum. The ointment should help you free her from prison. Once that's accomplished, you both slip back under the cloak, undetected.'

Arjun blew into his palms. He knew very well it was never going to be that easy. 'We need to come up with a backup plan, just in case,' he said, chewing the end of his lip.

'That would make sense, especially since we don't know the terrain of Paschimi Ilaka.'

Bodhidharma nodded. 'Before we do that, there's one thing I want to warn you about. When you're in Lobhvan, do not wish for anything. Because once you do, it's extremely difficult to stop. You could be trapped in the forest of temptations forever.'

Thus prepared, but still quite anxious, Arjun began his journey cautiously through Lobhvan. The trees were tall and bulbous, their branches spiralling out like hands with outstretched fingers. The strange part, though, was that there was not a single leaf in sight, not even dried ones on the forest floor. The skies above had turned indigo, and the silvery beams that were streaming through the intertwined branches gave off a ghostly glow. It was the stillness, however, that was the most unnerving.

Arjun was about halfway through when he remembered Bodhidharma's warning. The very thought, unfortunately, reminded him of something he had wanted for a long time. And the very next moment, he had wished for a remote-controlled car.

Before Arjun could even think about what he had done, a variety of remote-controlled cars began to pop up on the cupped branches. He turned excitedly to the bright red one with fancy headlights that had materialized above his head. Arjun was about to slide out of the backpack to reach for the car when a faint memory of his mission to save the queen of hearts pulled him back. He somehow managed to draw in his fingers before curling them tightly into a fist.

The spell was broken.

In an instant, all the cars vanished without a trace. Arjun heaved a sigh of relief. It had been a close call indeed. He began to hum a tune to distract himself as he raced through the forest. Before long, he had reached its border with Paschimi Ilaka. He would have to be extra careful from here on.

When Arjun parted the branches, the sight that met his eyes shot a sickening feeling down his stomach. Paschimi Ilaka was covered with prickly black bushes and enveloped in a layer of smoke that gave off a putrid odour. In the distance stood a massive fort built of grey stone, its gloomy vine-covered towers rising towards the fetid skies. This was Veeran Gadh, the seat of Dushtasura's power.

Arjun pulled the cloak of invisibility over his head and stepped onto the path he had spotted, careful to keep his nose above the stench. He walked softly on the deserted track, keeping his eyes peeled for Dushtasura's guards. He soon drew close to the imposing fort. But as Arjun ran past, his cloak got tangled in a thorny patch and fell off. And just at that moment, Dushtasura's burly asura guards appeared.

Poor Arjun found himself facing two asura guards. They had turnip-like faces, with red slits for eyes and large nostrils sitting on pug noses. They had two tiny horns on their heads and sharp broken teeth that curved upwards from inside their thick lips. The guards wore bulky armour and carried heavy wooden maces that had barbed wire wound around them.

'What business do you have here?' shouted one of the guards.

Arjun's voice died in his throat at the sudden turn of events. The guards approached menacingly, holding up their maces. Arjun stood his ground, however, looking right at them. Although rivulets of perspiration were flowing down his back, he couldn't afford to betray his fear. It was time to put the backup plan into action.

'I've been sent by the badshahs of Tashkot,' he said, pulling himself up. 'I bring with me the four royal sceptres. Take me to your king.'

The guards grabbed Arjun by his arms and whisked him away to the fort, which was surrounded by a deep, water-filled moat that was home to fierce black crocodiles. They crossed the drawbridge and were soon standing before Dushtasura, a fierce asura covered in thick, black hide from head to toe with deep, hardened grooves pointing outwards. He had long ram-like horns protruding from his skull, and eyes that glowed like red embers from below the ridge-like eyebrows. 'Why do you waste my time with this human child?' his voice thundered through his sharp, reptilian teeth.

'I bear the four sceptres of Tashkot,' croaked Arjun, trying to hold his trembling hands steady.

Dushtasura leaned forward, straddling his throne. 'So the badshahs of Tashkot hide in the shadows of a mere child,' he smirked. A nasty grin spread across his thin lips. 'Relieve him of the bag and throw him into the tower. Now that I have the sceptres, I will need to think up some more demands.'

Arjun found himself being marched up a spiral staircase that ran up the slimy stone walls of the tallest tower, for the better part of an hour, before the guards finally pushed him into a cell. When he turned around, he found himself looking at the tear-stained face of the queen of hearts, illuminated by the faint light that filtered in through the small window on one side. She had been imprisoned inside a circular glass chamber right at the centre.

'I've been sent to rescue you,' said Arjun, before running over to the window. Thick vines grew all the way down the side. And stretched out in front of him, as far as the eye could see, was the forest of temptations.

'They've sent a human child,' wailed Paan Ki Begum, alarm writ large on her delicate face. She pushed her palms against the glass. 'How can you rescue me if you've been caught as well?'

'It was certainly not a calculated move, but I can tell you it's probably the luckiest thing that's happened to me today,' said Arjun, removing the small bottle from his trouser pocket. 'I wasn't sure how I'd find you. But Dushtasura himself has made it possible.'

'What's that?' asked the queen.

'It's a spell to open the door,' said Arjun, dabbing some of the green substance on the lock. But the lock only sputtered. Even when he applied some more, the lock only gave a little gasp but still did not open. 'Why isn't this working?' he cried in alarm.

Paan Ki Begum pressed her back against the glass. 'Spells from Chamatkar Nagri don't always work properly here.'

Arjun's lips had gone dry. In a last-ditch effort, he removed a large blob of the ointment and smeared it on the lock. The lock coughed a few times before finally clicking open. The queen of hearts ran out. 'What do we do now?' she asked.

'There's no ointment left for the main door,' said Arjun, looking down at the empty bottle glumly. He leaned over the window. 'We could climb down these

vines. They look quite stable.'

But Paan Ki Begum gave a little shriek. 'I'm afraid of heights.'

Arjun rubbed his knuckles together, his gaze fixed upon the dark corner by the window. 'I have a plan,' he said, nodding slowly. 'I want you to hide in the shadows. And please don't make a sound.'

Paan Ki Begum slipped into the shadows while Arjun knocked on the door from inside.

A small iron window slid open. 'What do you want?' barked the guard. But he didn't wait for an answer, as his eyes fell upon the empty glass chamber. He hurriedly fumbled with the keys. Moments later, the door crashed open and the guard ran into the chamber. Arjun signalled Paan Ki Begum to get out of the room, and in one smooth movement, he slammed the door shut, locking the guard inside.

Arjun and Paan Ki Begum ran down the spiral staircase. They tiptoed to a halt when they saw a couple of hefty shadows at the entrance. Paan Ki Begum raised her eyebrows, but Arjun had already sprung into action. He chucked a small pebble at the guard on the right, catching him squarely on the cheek.

'Hey, quit that,' the guard snarled, rubbing his cheek.

'What?' the other guard yelled.

The first guard simply glared at him and stared ahead once again. But Arjun was ready. He launched another pebble and hit the second guard on his ear. This guard was in a surly mood and threw himself upon his companion. As they rolled over the cold stone stairs, Arjun caught hold of Paan Ki Begum's hand and shot across the drawbridge towards the prickly bushes where the cloak of invisibility had fallen off.

But Dushtasura had spotted them from his abode in the tower. A blood-curdling cry rose from his gnarled throat, followed by flashes of red lightning bolts from his wand. The spells fell like a shower of meteors and singed the bushes. But it was too late. Arjun and Paan Ki Begum had already dived under the cloak of invisibility.

'Don't wish for anything,' shouted Arjun, as they dashed into Lobhvan.

'Dushtasura had called,' smiled Bhadradharma. 'He proclaimed himself supreme ruler of Tashkot. I asked him to enjoy the sceptres since they were made of cheese.'

Everyone laughed. Things were back to normal in Chamatkar Nagri again.

Paan Ki Begum jumped into the arms of her badshah upon their return, tears streaming down her tired face. Everyone thumped Arjun's back heartily. But Anindita was the happiest of all. She had been afraid that her brother would be turned into a black beetle.

'It's time the children returned to Manav Lok,' said Bhadradharma, as Arjun yawned next to him. He drew out his wand and twirled it around, conjuring a house of cards around them. Before they could blink, the cards fell down and they found themselves sitting on their bed.

Anindita quickly found the queen of hearts. The picture was back. 'Thank you, children,' she said, winking at them.

The Chakora's Egg

'It's extremely urgent,' pleaded the yaksha. 'I must talk to Maharaj right away.'

'This is Nidrakhand, the land of sleep,' yawned the guard. 'I'm not even allowed to wake up Raja Vishramaditya during the two hours of daylight we get. How do you expect me to disturb him when it's dark outside?'

'If you don't wake him up, there may not even be a Chamatkar Nagri soon,' cried the yaksha, jumping around frantically in his red dhoti.

Suddenly, there was a loud crash behind the tall mahogany door that had a moon-like shape on its surface. It sounded like someone had fallen out of his bed. 'Now you've done it,' wailed the guard. 'Raja Vishramaditya will turn us both into sloths.'

The King of Nidrakhand threw open the door and tottered out, a dark look clouding his round face. 'Who dares awaken me in the middle of the night?' he thundered, his eyes blazing with anger. A series of quick yawns followed.

'I offer my humble apologies, Maharaj,' squeaked the yaksha, 'but this was something that couldn't wait. The Mahanagri Parishad has received word from our friends in adjoining Chakorpat that an egg has been stolen.'

Raja Vishramaditya was suddenly wide awake. 'What, what ... where ... how

... this is very serious,' he sputtered, almost falling over. 'What did Shwetvardhan say? Have the other kings been alerted? Who could have done this?'

'It was stolen by Keechad, a pishacha who escaped from prison a year ago. The chakoras did give chase, but he managed to escape into Manav Lok. And chakoras cannot enter Manav Lok because of an ancient spell.'

The King of Nidrakhand frowned. 'But why would a pishacha steal a chakora's egg?'

'I'm afraid there's more bad news, Maharaj. Shwetvardhan, the respected elder, also received some information from our spies in the northern regions. One of them overheard a conversation between Jadugarni Ghrunadasi and Keechad, in which she promised him 50 gold mudras if he stole a chakora's egg.'

Raja Vishramaditya reached for the door to steady himself. This was worse than he had thought. 'Ghrunadasi is Krooradasa's sister, whom my good friend—Raja Balushahi—turned into a piece of dry toast. She has vowed to take revenge against Chamatkar Nagri. If she gets her hands on a chakora's egg, she can use it to concoct all sorts of powerful evil spells that can wreak havoc upon our land. We must stop her at any cost.'

'But Maharaj, Keechad has entered Manav Lok. And our spies have received news that Ghrunadasi has crossed into Patala.'

Raja Vishramaditya shuddered at the mention of Patala. It was a frightful place, full of vast bogs filled with mud that was teeming with deadly scorpions. Cold winds, which sounded like weeping banshees, swept across the cursed lands. But there was something else too. The swampland was home to the bhootas, evil spirits that remained wrapped around kankaal trees, thus named because of their skeletal structures.

'How are we going to get out of this one?' the king muttered to himself.

Meanwhile, in Manav Lok ...

Anindita was sitting in the garden at the back of the house, rubbing her feet gently against the soft blades of grass. She had just finished playing school with her dolls and was wondering what to do next. Arjun was still fast asleep after a late night of helping Dadi clean the attic.

'I know,' smiled Anindita, picking up her favourite doll, Radha. 'Let's have a cookout.'

As she got busy with her kitchen set, she did not notice a pair of greyish-green eyes staring at her from behind one of the bushes. It was none other than the rogue pishacha.

As luck would have it, Keechad had slipped into their garden to flee the chakoras. Realizing that it wasn't possible to carry the egg around, he had buried it under a pile of dry grass in the corner and snuck out to receive further instructions from Ghrunadasi. But when he returned, he had been horrified to see a human child just a few feet away from his plunder.

As Keechad hid in the bushes, trying to figure out how to get to the egg, a gust of wind blew in from the west and swept away some of the blades of grass. Anindita shielded her face instinctively, but from the corner of her eye, she glimpsed something bright blue.

'Arjun! Look what I found,' she shouted, picking up the egg.

'That belongs to me,' said a coarse voice from behind her, as Keechad had stepped out of his hiding place.

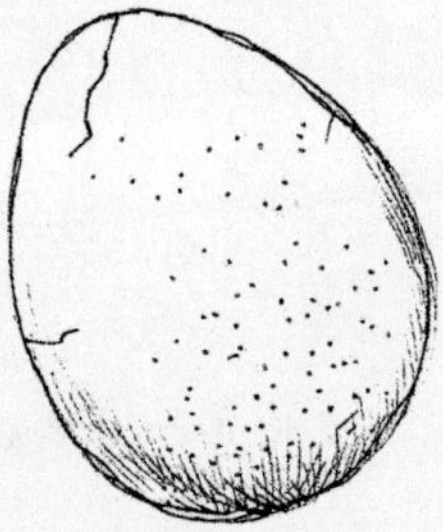

Anindita was surprised to see the small bald creature. He had protruding eyes, flared nostrils and yellowed fangs that stuck out from under his rough lips. But the most striking feature was his feet, which were like those of a goat.

'Give me the egg,' said Keechad, clopping his hooves impatiently.

Anindita narrowed her eyes. 'I don't think this belongs to you.'

The pishacha decided to change his approach. 'If you give me the egg,' he said, giving her a sly smile, 'I will give you a gold mudra.'

'I don't want your mudra. I'm not giving you this egg.'

'Then I shall take it from you!' screeched Keechad, walking towards her menacingly.

Anindita suddenly felt scared. 'Arjun, help ... help,' she screamed, clutching the egg tightly.

Arjun was already up but had decided to laze around in bed for a few extra minutes. When he heard his sister's frantic cries, he jumped out of bed and ran to the window.

But it was too late. Keechad had already muttered a spell, and he saw them both vanish in a wisp of black smoke.

Arjun darted outside, but all that remained was a few broken blades of grass and Radha, Anindita's favourite doll, lying face down. He pounded the ground with his fists, hot tears pouring down his cheeks. Just then, something fluttered nearby, distracting him. It was a torn piece of paper. Arjun picked it up. It had two words scribbled on it: Bhayankar Gadh.

There was no time to think. Arjun had to find a way back to Chamatkar Nagri. And the only place he could think of was the woods. But would the door be there? He dearly hoped it had returned from its sojourn. Arjun heaved a sigh of relief when he found it tucked away in a secluded part by the stream. But there was a tiny detail still missing. The last time they had crossed, a laddoo had made it all possible.

Arjun clasped the knob and tugged at it. But the door did not budge. He was about to punch the wood, when words began to magically appear on the front.

Yawn once and take a breath deep
Then jump, jump into the sand
In time you shall drift off to sleep
And dream your way into slumber land.

As soon as Arjun took a deep breath, the door fell flat with a dull thud, revealing the sandpit below. He jumped in without a second thought. But instead of plummeting downwards, he found himself floating like a leaf. Arjun's eyelids soon grew heavy amidst the rhythmic rocking motion and the soothing sound of the sand slipping down the sides. He dreamt of being carried upon a soft, silvery cloud, across azure seas and mystical islands, and over towering mountains and hidden vales.

When Arjun woke up, he found himself surrounded by slender gandharvas chattering excitedly. 'That was a strange dream,' he started to say, only to realize that he was actually lying on a cloud. When he sat up, he was treated to a panoramic view of Nidrakhand.

The entire place was covered with vast expanses of green, connected by serene lakes that glistened in the twilight. In the distance, on top of a gently sloping hill, was a sprawling white palace, its many towers topped with silver domes that were illuminated by a faint moon. The magnificent palace cast a benevolent shadow upon the many silver domed houses that dotted the landscape below. But the most captivating feature of Nidrakhand was the clouds, spread over the entire land like a blanket of snow. The clouds rested upon the domes, lingered around the branches, wandered along the banks or drifted aimlessly across the skies.

Arjun stretched his arms out and yawned again. 'I thought this was slumber land,' he said groggily. 'Why is there so much noise?'

'Haven't you heard?' said one of the gandharvas excitedly. He was floating on an adjacent cloud. 'A pishacha named Keechad stole an egg from Chakorpat and slipped into Manav Lok. And there are rumours that he plans to give it to the Jadugarni Ghrunadasi to use against Chamatkar Nagri.'

Arjun's ears perked up at this piece of information. He had been wondering how to start his search for Anindita. But the door had obviously known. 'You must take me to your king immediately,' he pleaded. 'I think I know where the pishacha is headed. He's kidnapped my sister as well.'

The gandharvas pushed the cloud—upon which Arjun was perched—towards the palace. 'Why am I still feeling so sleepy?' said Arjun, as the breeze ruffled his hair. He had half a mind to fluff a pillow out of the cloud and lie down again.

The gandharvas smiled. 'It's the wind,' said one of them. 'It moves around Nidrakhand whispering sweet lullabies.'

Arjun listened closely. They were right. He rubbed his eyes and blinked them repeatedly. This wasn't the time to nap.

A guard rushed forward as the clouds descended near the palace grounds. 'Who goes there?' he cried, raising his spear.

'He has information about Keechad,' chanted the gandharvas.

'Raja Vishramaditya is in conference with Shwetvardhan, the respected elder, and Chandraveera, King of the Chakoras,' said the guard, leading the way.

They soon reached the beautiful palace garden, bursting with the calming fragrance of water lilies. Wisps of clouds glided around on the light wind that continued to hum soothing melodies. Arjun stifled a yawn as he stepped into the tranquil shadows.

He could see two silhouettes under the towering presence of a gigantic bird, who was but obviously Chandraveera, King of the Chakoras. The Chakora King was easily over 50 feet tall, with beautiful white feathers that cascaded down his magnificent wings, ending in a plume of long feathers that swayed elegantly in the wind. His head ended in a beak that was sharp enough to break large boulders. Arjun was fascinated by his tail, which flowed from his body like a comet, leaving a trail of shooting stars.

'You must be Arjun,' said Shwetvardhan, stepping out of the shadows. 'This was the human child I was telling you about, Vishram. But how did you know we were in trouble?'

'I didn't,' replied Arjun, his lips quivering. 'My sister has been kidnapped by a pishacha. I caught a glimpse of a round blue thing before they disappeared. I assume that's the egg everyone's talking about.'

Raja Vishramaditya's round face clouded over with concern. 'If they have your sister, we must tread very carefully,' he said. He then told Arjun about everything that had happened so far.

'Ghrunadasi is Krooradasa's sister!' Arjun gulped. Things were beginning to look quite bleak.

'We have till midnight to recover the chakora's egg, before the third moon of Chamatkar Nagri turns blue,' sighed Shwetvardhan. 'If we fail, Chamatkar Nagri may cease to exist.'

'I wish I had stopped the pishacha before he jumped into Manav Lok,' said Chandraveera in a deep voice. 'What can we do?'

'I'm not sure,' replied Raja Vishramaditya, before taking a long drawn-out yawn. 'Sorry, force of habit. The truth is, we don't know where the egg or Ghrunadasi is right now.'

Arjun fished out the piece of paper from his pocket. 'I found this at the place they disappeared,' he said, handing it to Shwetvardhan.

'Bhayankar Gadh,' read out the elder. 'I should have known. It's Krooradasa's fort.'

'Now that you know where she is, can you stop her?' asked Arjun impatiently. He couldn't bear the thought of his sister languishing in some dark prison.

But Shwetvardhan shook his head. 'It's not going to be that simple,' he said, sighing. 'Bhayankar Gadh is very close to Patala. Just like the Paschimi Ilaka, our spells become weaker as we get closer to the land of beyond. Unfortunately, Ghrunadasi's spells become even more powerful.'

'As I see it, our only chance would be to sneak inside the fort and get the egg,' said Raja Vishramaditya.

'Along with Anindita,' added Arjun.

'Absolutely. I'm quite sure she's fine, at least for now. Ghrunadasi will be busy with preparations for midnight.'

'I don't think we should waste any more time,' said Chandraveera. 'I shall fly you all to the fort immediately. If we don't get the egg back, the very existence of Chakorpat will be threatened. A chakora's egg is laid only once every decade.'

'Then let's be on our way,' said Shwetvardhan, rising up in the air and descending slowly upon Chandraveera's back, even as Arjun and Raja Vishramaditya floated by his side upon a cloud. 'It's going to be a long night.'

The chakora king dipped his sharp talons and soared into the cobalt skies, flapping his mighty wings so hard that the clouds around the palace burst outwards with an explosive force. They travelled through the cover of darkness, gliding above the bed of clouds until they were suddenly surrounded by a putrid wind blowing from the other side. Bhayankar Gadh was nearby.

'Don't get too close to the fort,' shouted Shwetvardhan in Chandraveera's ear. 'It would be better if we landed in Banjarvan.'

The chakora king swooped down, breaking through the white mass. He moved swiftly towards a large tract of serene but dead forest and landed upon an open stretch near the edge. Beyond the forest stood Krooradasa's fort, rising high into a vortex of grey clouds that swirled around menacingly.

Shwetvardhan parted the lifeless branches and peered through the maze of large boulders that were scattered for miles. In the far distance, the terrain merged with a tide of sludge. This was Patala.

'What does Ghrunadasi plan to do?' asked Arjun.

'The two most important components of the spell are the egg and the blue rays of the third moon,' replied Shwetvardhan. 'But that's all I know.'

'Is there any way to block the rays of the moon?' asked Chandraveera.

The elder stared at the moon before shaking his head summarily. 'The rays are magical and will pass through anything,' he said. 'Perhaps I can do something about the egg once we're inside. Chandraveera, I want you to remain hidden here. Be ready to take off the moment we're out.' He turned to the others and continued, 'This is a very dangerous place. So please be vigilant.'

As the chakora king merged into the night, Arjun, Raja Vishramaditya and Shwetvardhan entered the labyrinth of boulders. Everything was deathly still, cold and morbid. Soon, they were standing near the mouth of Bhayankar Gadh. With its tall towers, jagged edges and carvings of demons that stared down accusingly, the place had an evil aura that seemed to burn into their skins.

'How do we get past those guards?' asked Raja Vishramaditya, peering at the bulky silhouettes of the rats with long, creepy tails that were gliding around the fort.

Shwetvardhan drew a circle around them with his wand. 'This is a very powerful spell and should work here,' he said, before chanting under his breath.

All of a sudden, the circle began to expand. But it was actually the three of them who were getting smaller and smaller. By the time Arjun could catch his breath, they were all the size of mice.

'The moon,' said Raja Vishramaditya, sighing. Its rays had turned a pale blue. 'The transformation has started. We have only about an hour.'

The trio crawled under the door softly and soundlessly. The fort was submerged in darkness, but they spotted a patch of light emerging from under a door at one corner of the fort. When they came closer, they realized that the crackling and sizzling sounds from behind the door meant that Ghrunadasi was busy making final preparations for the spell.

'Listen,' whispered Raja Vishramaditya, closing his eyes. He pointed to a door on his right. 'I hear someone sobbing in there.'

'It must be Anindita.'

Shwetvardhan caught hold of his hand. 'We must be careful. If she's inside, Keechad could be there as well.'

They crept under the door and tiptoed through the shadows until they were lodged safely inside a crack in the stone wall. When they peeped out, they saw Anindita sobbing quietly in a corner. Keechad sat on a chair nearby, his tired eyes glued to the egg that was lying on a bed of hay in front of him. They could also see the moon through the window. Its rays had turned a darker shade of blue.

'I must try something.' Shwetvardhan removed his wand and began to chant under his breath, his eyes fixed upon the egg. But he stopped a few minutes later and shook his head. 'Ghrunadasi has put a lot of dark enchantments over the fort. My spells have grown very weak.'

'What will happen if the egg is gone?' asked Arjun, chewing his lips.

'But Shwetvardhan can't even move it,' groaned Raja Vishramaditya.

Arjun smiled wryly. 'He doesn't need to. I've got an idea.'

He crawled out from the crack and leapt right in front of the egg, waving his arms wildly and shouting at the top of his voice. Keechad, who was about to nod off, sat up when he heard Anindita's shriek of delight. And that's when he saw Arjun dancing around wildly. The pishacha stumbled out of his seat, but by then, Arjun had already scrambled out from under the door.

As Keechad chased Arjun on his stumpy goat feet, Raja Vishramaditya and Shwetvardhan ran over to Anindita. 'Cover the egg with lots of hay,' shouted the elder. 'We don't have much time.'

Anindita jumped up and started to pile hay upon the egg as the others removed their wands and began to chant under their breath. Once Anindita was done, Raja Vishramaditya shouted, 'Put us inside your pocket, quickly! Someone's coming.'

It was Keechad, returning after an unsuccessful attempt to capture Arjun. He had decided against mentioning anything to Ghrunadasi.

Just then, the jadugarni's rasping voice shot out from her chamber. 'Get me the egg now, carefully. If anything happens to it, I shall feed you to my rats. And bring the girl as well.'

Keechad glared at Anindita, too shaken to say anything. He picked up the egg cautiously, his fingers trembling. He had failed to notice that the egg was now covered with hay. The inside of Ghrunadasi's chamber was dimly lit with candles that emitted an eerie, blue light. A large, black circle inscribed with strange markings had been drawn in chalk on the cold floor. And at the centre stood the stumpy, hunchbacked figure of the jadugarni, in black garb. She had a hooked nose, a face full of warts and eyes that were the same rabid yellow as her brother's. Through a window on top, a stream of dark blue light fell upon her mop of dirty, straw-like hair. 'Do you know what I'm going to do?' she cackled. 'I'm going to turn Chamatkar Nagri into a big piece of rotten cheese and send my army of rats to eat it up.'

Keechad clapped in delight even as the occupants of Anindita's pocket squirmed. Arjun, who was hiding in the shadows, felt a shiver go down his spine.

Ghrunadasi held up the blue egg in her bony fingers and raised it high above her head, blocking out the moon's rays. Her eyes rolled back into their sockets as she began to chant in a throaty voice. Moments later, the circle and the markings around her burst into a demonic fire. The moon had turned a sordid blue, the colour that spelt doom for Chamatkar Nagri.

Suddenly, Shwetvardhan nudged his companion, pointing towards the egg. A tiny crack had appeared. 'So Arjun's idea did work,' sighed Raja Vishramaditya. 'Do you know the first thing ...?'

But he didn't get a chance to complete his sentence. The egg cracked open, and a tiny, white chakora emerged. It snorted gently before sending out a violent burst of flames at her captor, setting her robes ablaze. A loud wail erupted from the jadugarni's bulging lips. But the dark enchantments had been broken. Ghrunadasi's wand moved swiftly through the air, whisking her entire contingent away to Patala in a cloud of smoke.

Back in Nidrakhand, Chandraveera cradled the baby chakora, who was now fast asleep. Chamatkar Nagri was safe once again.

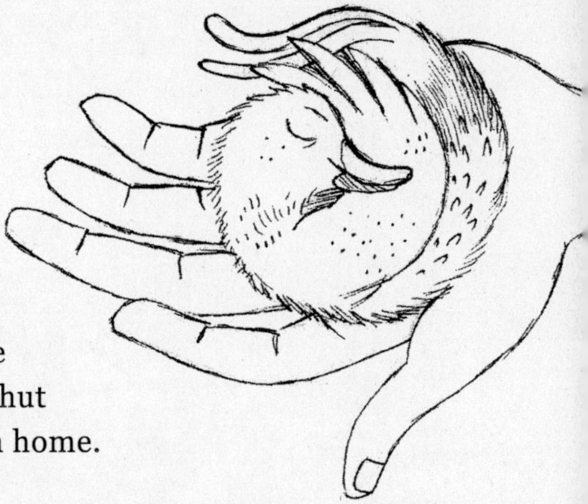

Raja Vishramaditya managed to express his gratitude to Arjun in between loud yawns. Moments later, he drifted off to sleep.

Shwetvardhan smiled at the children. 'It's been a long day for the two of you,' he said, waving his wand through the air. A cool breeze swirled around them, caressing their eyes shut before picking them up gently and carrying them home.

When Arjun and Anindita opened their eyes the next morning, they found themselves in bed. Anindita threw her arms around her brother. 'Thanks for saving me,' she cried. 'I was so scared when that pishacha took me to Bhayankar Gadh. Such a pity that Keechad and Ghrunadasi got away.'

Arjun squeezed her hand. 'I'm just glad you're fine. And I have a feeling those two will be back. When they do, we'll be ready for them.'

Aladdin's Lamp

'I tried to grant his wish, but all I got was a poof and a wisp of smoke,' said the plump jinn, pulling in his broad shoulders. 'I felt so ashamed when the little boy laughed at me.'

'I know exactly how you feel,' sighed a jinn in the front row. 'I couldn't even conjure up a simple ice-cream cone. It was so heartbreaking to watch the little girl cry.'

The plump jinn looked up in alarm. 'What if we can never grant wishes again?' he gulped. Even the thought was horrifying.

There was a major crisis in Jinntara. For the past two days, the jinns hadn't been able to grant wishes to children from Manav Lok. There was a rumour going around that someone had been stealing wishes from Divyakosh, the repository of wishes. The Mahanagri Parishad had been alerted, but even the elders had drawn a blank as to why the jinns were unable to grant wishes. Such a thing had never happened before.

Sultan Ali, the King of Jinntara, had convened an emergency meeting in the main chamber of Chirag Mahal. After hearing a few of the jinns, he spoke in a calm, firm voice. 'A calamity of this nature has never befallen our land.

However, panic is not going to solve our problems. The Mahanagri Parishad is trying to find out if any dark force is behind this. Meanwhile, I have also received word that the great Abu is on his way to the palace.'

Abu, the most powerful jinn in Jinntara, had been in deep meditation for the past thousand years. It was forbidden to disturb him unless the circumstances were grave. Unfortunately, this time they were. Sultan Ali had sent a message to the jinn masters to awaken Abu, who had been resting deep inside a mountain cave in the heart of Jinntara.

'Hail the great Abu. May his wisdom guide us.' A chant rose in the air as a golden jinn sailed into the chamber, leaving behind a trail of shimmering mist. He had a towering presence that was accompanied by a commanding yet gentle aura.

Even as the jinns bowed in respect, Abu said, with a deep frown on his forehead, 'I knew what the problem was the moment I was awakened.'

Sultan Ali ushered Abu to the throne. 'But why aren't we able to grant wishes?' he asked.

'It was prophesized many thousands of years ago that when the fifth moon over Chamatkar Nagri falls exactly in line with the first moon, Ichchavadh shall rise and steal our wishes.'

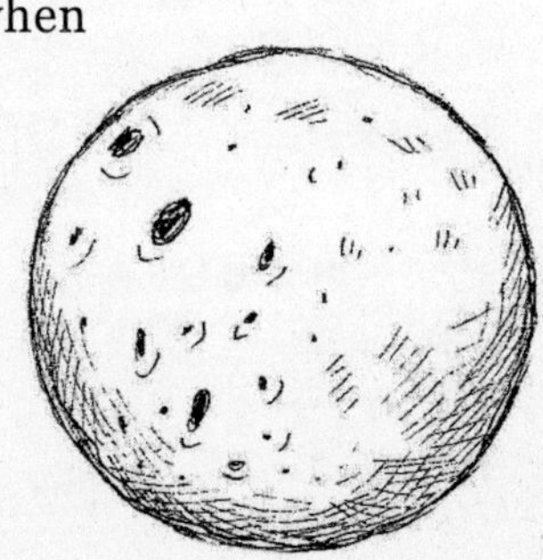

The jinns began to chatter agitatedly.

Abu raised his hand. 'According to my calculations, Ichchavadh would have emerged a couple of days ago.'

'So how do we stop him?' asked Sultan Ali, even as the other jinns looked on hopefully.

Abu stroked his beard, staring vacantly at the polished walls. He finally shook his head and said in a sombre voice, 'There's nothing we can do.'

A hushed silence fell over the jinns in the chamber. The jinns had assumed that Abu would have the answer to the problem that was plaguing Jinntara.

'The prophecy, however, does say that the answer shall arrive from Manav Lok.'

Meanwhile, in Manav Lok ...

Arjun and Anindita had just reached home after spending an evening at the second-hand shop in the village. They had sifted through mountains of old books piled up against the peeling walls. They had rummaged through the quaint curios on the broken shelves around the room. And they had raised a storm of dust digging through the boxes in the back. After their recent encounter with Ghrunadasi, it had felt good to spend a quiet day in the heart of the peaceful village.

'I can't understand why you would buy an old lamp,' said Arjun, placing the model car he had picked out on the chest of drawers. He admired it for a few moments before facing his sister with raised eyebrows.

'I think it's pretty,' said Anindita, trying to see her reflection on its surface. But the lamp had dulled over time. She rubbed it instinctively against her dress to clean up the dust. The lamp glistened under the glow of the yellow light, revealing an intricate design. But before she could take a closer look, a wisp of red smoke suddenly shot out of its spout.

'What happened?' asked Arjun, as she threw the lamp aside in a hurry.

'I ... I think I saw some smoke.'

'It must be the dust.' Arjun picked up the lamp and rolled it gently against the light. 'There's some writing on the other side.'

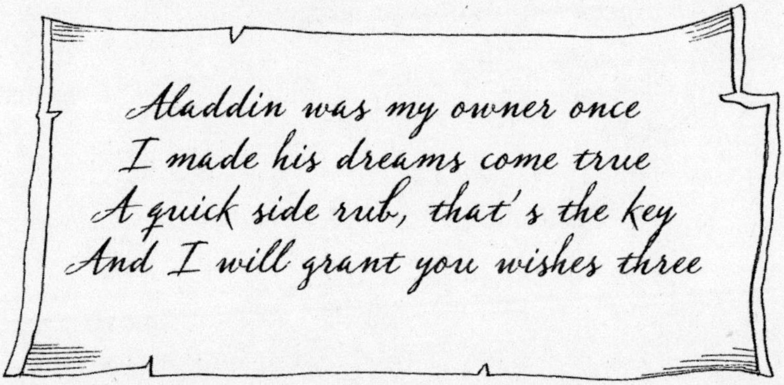

'It's Aladdin's lamp,' exclaimed Anindita, unable to contain her excitement.

'Looks like it,' said Arjun.

Anindita began to pace the floor. 'We've only got three wishes. So let's make a list first. I've always wanted a ...'

'Something's wrong.'

'What do you mean?'

'Didn't you just rub the lamp?'

Anindita stopped in her tracks. 'I did, didn't I?' she said in a small voice.

'Perhaps you didn't do it properly,' said Arjun, seeing her disappointed face. 'Why don't you try again?'

Anindita curled her fingers delicately around the elaborate handle and gave the side of the lamp a vigorous rub. But all they got was another wisp of red smoke. The children looked at each other before trying to peer down the spout. Suddenly, a large puff of smoke shot out, wrapping itself around them like a cocoon and rising up swiftly. It sucked them up with such force that they both got dragged along.

'My head hurts,' groaned Arjun, kneading the flat of his thumb into his right temple. When he looked around, he found himself lying on a large four-poster bed covered with delicately netted golden drapes. Beyond the drapes, something appeared to be floating back and forth. Anindita stirred at his side. 'Where are we?' she asked, struggling to open her eyes.

The drapes parted, and a genial golden being appeared. 'Please drink this nectar,' he said, handing goblets to the children. 'It will clear up your headache. I shall explain everything later.'

Arjun and Anindita sipped the nectar, which tasted like a mixture of raw mangoes and sugarcane with a dash of ginger and saffron. Before long, they were feeling fresh and energetic.

'I'm Abu, the golden jinn,' said the golden being, 'and you're inside my house in Jinntara.'

'Do you stay inside the lamp?' asked Arjun, unable to contain his curiosity. He had a distinct recollection of being pulled inside.

Abu nodded. ‘Actually, every dwelling in Jinntara has a passage to a lamp in Manav Lok. Whenever a child rubs a lamp, the jinn who belongs to that lamp emerges and grants three wishes. The lamp in your possession is Aladdin’s lamp, and I’m the jinn of the lamp.’

‘We didn’t get any wishes,’ said Anindita in a small voice.

Abu looked away, crestfallen. He then recounted the crisis that had befallen Jinntara.

Arjun couldn’t believe his ears. ‘But why have we been brought here?’

‘It’s destiny that has brought you here,’ said Abu. ‘Otherwise, you would never have found Aladdin’s lamp. It’s been lost for over a thousand years.’

Arjun could feel his heart thumping against his rib cage. 'So what can you tell us about Ichchavadh?' he asked, dearly hoping he was nothing like Krooradasa or Dushtasura.

'I'm only familiar with the anecdote that has been passed down by my forefathers. It was said that a jinn was cursed at the very beginning of time for failing to grant a wish – a jinn's sacred duty. According to the prophecy, Ichchavadh, the stealer of wishes, will awaken when the fifth moon of Chamatkar Nagri aligns with the first moon. This has already happened.'

'Does the prophecy say anything else?'

'Indeed, it does. But it shall only be revealed to beings from Manav Lok.' With this, Abu began to move his arms gently and rhythmically through the air, leaving behind magical trails of sparkling red. Moments later, a large crimson ruby materialized in the space between his golden palms.

As Arjun and Anindita looked closely, the stone suddenly became misty and golden words appeared inside. Arjun read them out.

When five and one shall align; the wishes
will cease to shine
The third one shall show the way; to the
Divine is linked its ray
Challenge the given, uncover the hidden
Only those who wish may try; else the
wishes will run dry
Not eternity, but half a day; to banish
the slayer of wishes away

'It's a puzzle,' exclaimed Anindita, as the stone turned to dust and blew away.

Arjun sat upon the bed, lost in thought. He enjoyed solving puzzles, but this was something completely different. And they only had half a day to work through it. 'Can you please tell us something more about the wishes?'

Abu crossed his arms solemnly. 'There are three sacred rules that govern the granting of wishes, rules that cannot be violated under any circumstances. First, a jinn can only grant wishes to a being from Manav Lok. Second, a jinn cannot grant wishes where harm is intended. Third, a jinn can only grant three wishes to the owner of the lamp, no more.'

'And what is this Divyakosh you mentioned earlier?' asked Anindita.

'It's where all the wishes are stored. The moment a wish is used up, another gets added into the Divyakosh instantly. But none of us know its workings. It's been functioning in this way for centuries, without any intervention.'

'Very interesting,' replied Arjun, scratching the tip of his ear. 'Anyway, let's start working on the prophecy now.'

'I believe it will be helpful if we call in Sultan Ali as well,' said Abu. 'He may be able to help us.'

As Abu drifted away, Anindita turned to her brother. 'Do you think we will be able to solve the puzzle?'

Arjun shrugged. 'I'm really not sure,' he sighed. 'Some lines seem straightforward, others quite vague. But I have a feeling that we really need to dig deep to get to their real meaning. Perhaps we shall succeed if we put our heads together.'

Just then, Abu returned with Sultan Ali. 'I'm honoured to be in your presence,' he said, bowing deeply. 'The fate of Jinntara rests in your hands now.'

Arjun nodded slowly. He knew that all the jinns had pinned their hopes on them. 'Let's start with the first line of the prophecy.'

'When five and one shall align; the wishes will cease to shine,' repeated Anindita from memory.

'I think it's quite obvious what that means. The "five" and "one" refer to the respective moons of Chamatkar Nagri. When they fall in line, the wishes shall be stolen by Ichchavadh from the Divyakosh.'

The jinns nodded.

'The third one shall show the way; to the Divine is linked its ray,' said Arjun, turning to the pad where he had noted the prophecy. 'The third what?'

'It has to be the third moon,' said Sultan Ali, after some thought. 'It's the most powerful moon over Chamatkar Nagri.'

'Yes, that does make sense,' agreed Arjun. 'I remember how Ghrunadasi was going to use the blue rays of the third moon to turn Chamatkar Nagri into rotten cheese.'

'To the Divine is linked its ray,' said Anindita, reading the second part. 'What could that mean?'

'Perhaps the third moon gets its power from some magical source,' shrugged Abu, raising his eyebrows.

Arjun moved to the window and stared at the large moon moving sedately across the indigo horizon. 'I'm not so sure about that,' he said, turning around with a shake of his head. 'I think the Divyakosh gets its supply of wishes from the third moon.'

The jinns looked at him in amazement. 'Of course,' exclaimed Sultan Ali. 'Divyakosh means storehouse of the Divine. So that is the Divine that is linked to the rays of the moon.'

Anindita squeezed her brother's hand with a proud smile.

'What does the next line say?' asked Abu, excited at the progress they were making.

'Challenge the given, uncover the hidden,' said Arjun, glancing at the pad. 'So we need to look beyond the obvious, perhaps something that we have been assuming so far. But what could it be?'

After almost half an hour, they had still not made any headway. Finally, Arjun blew into his palms and sat up. 'We're obviously missing something,' he said, facing Sultan Ali. 'I've already heard the story from Abu. But I think I'd also like to hear it from you. Can you please tell us everything that's happened over the past couple of days?'

Sultan Ali narrated the events over the next few minutes, and everyone listened intently.

'Why don't you appoint guards to protect the Divyakosh from Ichchavadh?' asked Anindita.

Before either of the jinns could respond, Arjun blurted out. 'That's it,' he cried, almost falling over in excitement. 'That's what we've been assuming all this while.'

'What do you mean?' asked Abu, with a confused look.

'Don't you see?' said Arjun. 'We've all been assuming that the Divyakosh is being robbed, since the jinns haven't been able to grant wishes to the children in Manav Lok. But I'm quite sure this isn't what's been happening.'

'But then, where are all the wishes disappearing?' asked Sultan Ali.

'I'm not yet sure,' replied Arjun, biting the side of his lip. 'But the one thing I'm certain about is that the Divyakosh has not been robbed,' he added confidently.

'How can you be so sure?' asked Abu.

Arjun drew a few squiggly lines in the air before bobbing his head decisively. 'Let me explain how things have been working before this problem started,' he said, measuring his words carefully. 'Whenever a jinn granted a wish, the third moon of Chamatkar Nagri would replace it in the Divyakosh. Which means that even if Ichchavadh were to steal a wish from the repository, the moon would immediately replace it.'

Abu closed his eyes. 'Yes, I do believe you're right,' he said a few moments later. 'We seem to have solved the part about challenging the given. Now we need to uncover the hidden.'

'We're still no closer to that because all we've done so far is eliminate one possibility. The hidden is quite obvious, but finding the right answer is going to be a very difficult task.' Arjun punched the bed in frustration. 'We don't have a clue about where the wishes are going. It just feels like we haven't made any progress at all.'

'That's not true,' smiled the wise Abu. 'But we have spent many hours pondering over the prophecy. It's time for a well-deserved break.'

'A very good idea indeed,' agreed Sultan Ali. 'It's almost daybreak. Let me take you around Jinntara.'

Jinntara was bathed in the warm glow and myriad colours of the early morning sun. The third moon no longer looked as ominous as it had a few hours earlier. Large golden lamps—home to the jinns—dotted the picturesque landscape. A thin mist moved slowly over the rolling plains, upon which they sat, and disappeared into the skies. It seemed like they were in a magical dream.

Anindita stared at her feet for a few moments, feeling the cold grass underneath. 'It's so pretty,' she sighed, as the mist swirled around, caressing her legs.

Arjun nodded absentmindedly. He was still lost in thought, trying to put together the pieces of the puzzle that were moving around in his head. They seemed to be playing a game of musical chairs with him. But just as he was about to give up, a faint pattern emerged, snapping him back to reality. 'That's

it,' he said, drawing his breath in sharply and startling his sister. 'I think I may just have found the answer. But I need to confirm something with Abu.'

The golden jinn looked worried when the trio burst in through the door. 'Is everything all right?'

'I need to know something,' said Arjun, after a hasty nod. 'You mentioned earlier that a jinn can only grant wishes to a being from Manav Lok. Does this mean that jinns cannot use the wishes themselves?'

'Yes, that's correct,' replied Abu. 'But how does that help us?'

Arjun exhaled slowly, his face relaxing into a wide grin. 'It's the last piece of the puzzle. I should have paid attention to the rules more closely.'

'Really?' exclaimed an ecstatic Sultan Ali.

'If you don't explain immediately, I will punch you,' said Anindita jestingly.

'We know for certain that the wishes are not being stolen from the Divyakosh in Jinntara. If they were, the third moon would simply replace them. So if they're not disappearing here, it can only mean they're getting lost in Manav Lok.'

Everyone nodded.

'Now, suppose there's no Ichchavadh, the slayer of wishes, the way we are imagining. I mean, suppose it's just a spell that cancels the wishes in Manav Lok. That will explain why the wishes are not working there.'

'That will explain a lot,' said Abu.

Arjun took a deep breath and continued. 'So if the wishes are not being stolen in Jinntara, why can't the jinns just wish the problem away? This is what I was wondering, when I remembered the first rule Abu had mentioned. That jinns can't use the wishes for themselves.'

'But then, how can we break the spell?' asked Sultan Ali impatiently.

'It's simple,' smiled Arjun. 'The second last line says, only those who wish may try. So who can wish? Children. But we also know that wishes are not working in Manav Lok at the moment. What do we do?'

Anindita started to jump excitedly. 'I know, I know,' she shouted. 'Since we rubbed Aladdin's lamp, we can make the wish. And since we're in Jinntara, not Manav Lok, our wish will work.'

'Exactly,' said Arjun, with a quiet look of satisfaction. It hadn't been easy by any measure, but he had managed to crack the riddle. 'And since you rubbed the lamp, you can make the wish.'

Anindita closed her eyes tightly. 'My first wish is that all the jinns should be able to grant wishes to children in Manav Lok from this moment on.'

'Your wish is my command,' said Abu, bowing deeply to her.

The instant Abu granted Anindita's first wish, things returned to normal in Jinntara. Loud shouts erupted from outside as the jinns realized their powers had been restored.

'So, would you like to use your remaining two wishes now, Anindita?' asked Abu, smiling at her.

'I don't think so,' replied Anindita, shaking her head slowly. She glanced at the celebrations unfolding outside. 'All the wishes I had thought of earlier seem to be so trivial compared to the wish I just made. I really want the other two wishes to count as well.'

'I was expecting nothing less from you,' said Abu. 'But it's now time to forget all our troubles and celebrate.'

Arjun and Anindita had a wonderful time with the jinns, dancing with them in the mist, zooming through the skies on their backs and sliding down the glittering lamps, before indulging in a lavish spread of magical goodies.

'It's time to go back,' said Abu, gently wrapping his large golden arms around the exhausted children. 'Jinntara will forever remain in your debt. And I remain at your command for the two wishes. All you have to do is rub the lamp.'

The golden jinn ushered them into his house as Sultan Ali and the jinns cheered loudly. Once inside, Abu waved his arms again, tracing magical patterns that left behind trails of red smoke. The smoke curled itself around the children, and before they knew what was happening, it had whisked them out of the spout.

They opened their eyes to the trills of early morning birds. It was a beautiful day, and sunshine poured into their bedroom.

'I really enjoyed this adventure,' yawned Arjun, stretching his arms out as far as he could.

'So did I,' said Anindita, bringing out the lamp from under the sheets. 'I wish I could go for another ride over Jinntara.'

Arjun put his palm to his mouth in mock alarm. 'Be careful what you wish for,' he winked. 'We have only two left.'

Anindita threw a pillow at him and burst out laughing.

Trouble In Khilonapatnam

A dark shadow had crept over Khilonapatnam, the land of toys. 'Our army is fully prepared to vanquish the kripa-kathors, Maharaj,' said Lohadil, a pompous wooden doll.

'I really wish there was a way to avoid this situation completely,' sighed Raja Tejbali, an old terracotta doll. 'There's been some monumental misunderstanding.'

Raja Tejbali, the King of Khilonapatnam, was discussing a very serious matter with his army chief, Lohadil. Someone had been stealing food from Kathorikripa, the neighbouring land. They had placed the blame squarely upon the khilonas and were now threatening to go to war.

Lohadil's face would have turned vermillion, had it not been painted a bright yellow. 'The time for diplomacy is over, Maharaj,' he declared, giving a sharp twist to the tip of his thick moustache. 'If they think they can hurl unsubstantiated accusations at us, they have another think coming. We shall defend the honour of Khilonapatnam with our dying breaths.'

'Perhaps we should ask the Mahanagri Parishad for assistance,' continued Raja Tejbali thoughtfully.

Lohadil clenched his fists silently. When he spoke, his voice was filled with bitterness. 'The Mahanagri Parishad would have rushed to our aid had it been Paschimi Ilaka. But in this case, they will only lecture us about the peace treaty between Kathorikripa and Chamatkar Nagri and ask us to solve the matter in a peaceful manner.'

'I'm all for a peaceful resolution,' said Raja Tejbali.

'But we've exhausted all options for peace, Maharaj,' protested the army chief. 'I've tried to reason with my Kathorikripa counterpart, but he refuses to believe that we're not responsible for the disappearance of their food.'

The King of Khilonapatnam sighed wearily. 'I won't send our forces into battle unless they attack. Just think about all the damage and destruction both lands will suffer if a war breaks out. It will be far worse than some missing food.'

Lohadil crossed his hands behind his back stubbornly. 'But they're the ones who're talking about confrontation, Maharaj. And it's unlikely they'll back down unless we provide solid evidence that Khilonapatnam doesn't have a hand in the disappearance of their food.'

'Do you believe an attack is imminent?' asked Raja Tejbali, his brow deeply furrowed.

'According to intelligence reports, they will initiate the assault within the next 24 hours,' replied Lohadil gravely.

Raja Tejbali squared his jaw. 'Very well, then,' he said in a steely voice, 'if a war is inevitable, then we shall not be caught unawares. Brief me about the preparations.'

'The soldiers along the border have been alerted, even as our trains are bringing in reinforcements. The cannons have been deployed at strategic locations to support the troops. And our plane squadrons are ready to depart at a moment's notice as well.'

'And what intelligence do you have about their military?'

Lohadil poured over the map spread upon the table. 'They've begun assembling soldiers along the border,' he replied, pointing at the precise locations. 'While they have a larger terrestrial army, we have aerial advantage.'

'Keep me updated on the hour,' said Raja Tejbali. He picked up a miniature cannon model and turned it around in his fingers. 'Only a miracle can save our lands now.'

Meanwhile, in Manav Lok ...

Arjun and Anindita were getting ready for bed after a tiring day spent helping out Dada in the garden.

'I really want to play with Radha,' sighed Anindita, falling upon the bed.

She flipped over and buried her face in the soft pillow. 'But I'm just so tired.'

'I think I'm going to do some reading,' said Arjun, reaching for the book on the small bedside table. For a moment, his eyes lingered on Aladdin's lamp shining next to it. 'I wonder where our next adventure will take us.'

There was a tiny snore from the other side. Anindita was already fast asleep.

Arjun smiled and opened the book. But about half an hour later, he too had nodded off and wandered into the world of dreams. He dreamt that he was chasing Keechad, the pishacha who had kidnapped Anindita, through a labyrinth of dark passages. Just as he was about to catch him, tapping sounds began to echo through the musty air, and the ground beneath his feet suddenly gave way.

Arjun woke up bathed in cold sweat. As the objects around him began to take shape, he realized it had only been a dream. He was about to close his eyes when he heard the tapping sounds again. But this time, they seemed real. Sitting up, he wondered if it could be a pari. 'Anindita, wake up,' he whispered, shaking her gently.

Anindita mumbled something in her sleep before turning over and pulling the blanket across her face.

'Wake up. There may be a pari in the attic.'

Anindita pushed aside the blanket and sat up, still drowsy and blinking from sleep. 'Did you say pari?' She yawned, stretching her arms out.

Arjun nodded and looked up. 'Do you hear that?'

'Are you sure it's not a mouse?' asked Anindita, with a slight shudder.

They slipped out of bed and tiptoed up to the attic with a torch. The sounds grew louder as they approached. They were accompanied by flashes of light that jumped out in waves through the partially open door.

Anindita turned to Arjun with raised eyebrows. 'There's only one way to find out,' he said. Then, exhaling softly, he pushed open the door.

The two of them were completely unprepared for the sight that awaited them. The floor of the dingy attic was filled with toys. A wooden elephant, a top, an electric train, a stuffed dog, papier-mache puppets, a plastic plane, soldier dolls, drums, blocks, balls and many other toys – all tooting and bouncing and spinning and jumping and zooming and chattering.

'The ... the toys are alive,' gulped Arjun.

Anindita nodded slowly. 'But whose toys are these?'

'They belonged to Daddy when he was growing up,' replied Arjun. He could see the large wooden box—now open—in which he had helped Dadi pack them up just days before. 'Isn't that Radha?' Arjun said, pointing in the distance.

Anindita looked in the direction of his finger. And sure enough, it was Radha, in a lively conversation with a Tanjore doll, who kept bobbing her head at everything.

The children would have continued gaping at the scene unfolding before them had one of the Rajasthani puppets in colourful red garb not spotted them in the shadows. 'We didn't mean to disturb you,' he said, after coughing loudly a few times to silence the other toys.

'What's happening here?' asked Arjun, still not sure that the puppet had actually spoken to him.

Radha stepped forward, her arms clasped together. 'We've just received news that our land may soon be going to war with Kathorikripa,' she cried. 'So word has been sent to all the toys in Manav Lok to reach Khilonapatnam at once. We really feel bad about this, but we must leave soon.'

Anindita stared at her doll for a few moments. Was Radha actually talking to her? 'Uh ... okay,' she finally managed to reply.

'But why are the toys going to war with Kathorikripa?' asked Arjun.

'We don't know,' squawked the bright green wooden parrot. 'But it's our duty to protect our land.'

A loud murmur of approval rose through the musty attic air.

'I'm not letting my dolls go into any battle alone,' said Anindita, pushing her chin up. 'We're coming with you.'

'Will you really help us?' asked the ball, rolling over.

'Of course,' replied Arjun.

Anindita's dolls rushed into her outstretched arms. 'Thank you ever so much,' they said in chorus.

'Where is Khilonapatnam?' asked Arjun. 'And how do we get there? Is there a door or something?'

'Khilonapatnam is a part of Chamatkar Nagri,' replied the grey stuffed dog.

'We shall take the elevator in the garden. But I do hope the ride isn't too bumpy this time.'

Anindita's jaw dropped to the floor. 'An elevator? In our garden?'

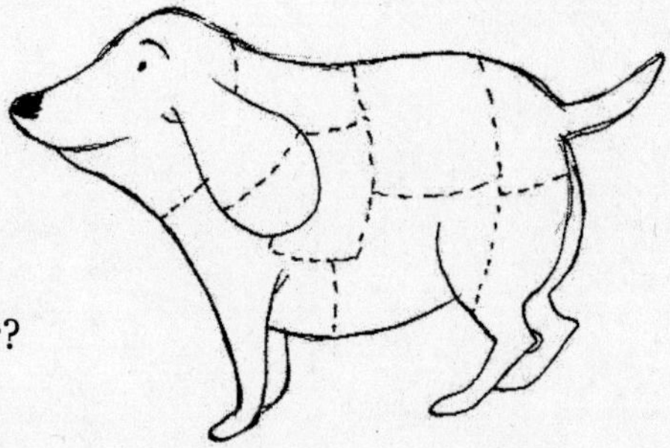

A warm breeze surrounded them as they all stepped out into the night. The thick cloud cover had immersed the village in darkness, but the bursts of light from the fireflies were just enough to guide them.

'There it is,' whispered one of the soldier dolls, pointing to a large ring of white mushrooms growing in the shade of an enormous tree nearby. 'Please get inside the circle.'

'I'm pretty sure it wasn't there this morning,' said Arjun.

'They only appear for an hour in the night.'

Everyone stepped in the ring. Arjun and Anindita's insides tingled with excitement as they waited in anticipation.

'Look for the largest mushroom,' said the dog, sniffing around the patch.

Radha found it moments later, hidden behind one of the roots. She nodded at the others and pushed it down.

Arjun and Anindita gasped for breath as the patch of grass shot downwards. It felt as though they were gliding down a long slide, like the one in the park back home. Only, this one had more twists and turns than a jalebi. And just as they were beginning to get used to the ride, they all popped out into Khilonapatnam from an opening in a plastic tree.

'That wasn't very pleasant,' groaned Arjun, rubbing his elbow, which had taken the impact of the fall.

'I didn't feel a thing,' said the ball, bouncing around happily.

When the children looked around, they felt like they had walked into the

world's largest toy store. Thousands upon thousands of toys had arrived from all corners of Manav Lok and assembled upon the streets of Khilonapatnam But the atmosphere was far from playful, for a pall of gloom had descended upon the place.

The heads of a papier-mache Ravana doll were discussing the matter amongst themselves nearby. Anindita overheard one of them making a case for finding a peaceful solution. *Exactly*, she thought. There had to be another way. 'We must stop this war,' she said, turning to Radha. 'Is there any way we can meet the King of Khilonapatnam?'

'Well, Jhuk Jhuk here used to be the king's royal train,' replied the doll. 'Perhaps he could take us to meet Raja Tejbali.'

'It was a long time ago,' sighed the electric train. But when he saw the pleading look in Anindita's eyes, he quickly added, 'We could certainly try, though.'

The electric train was soon speeding through the streets, with flashing lights and loud toots to make way through the crowd, as the children and the rest of their toys ran after it. Minutes later, they had reached the majestic palace of Raja Tejbali. But before they could go inside, they found themselves surrounded by the royal khilona guards.

'What do you want?' they growled.

'We need to meet the king urgently,' tooted Jhuk Jhuk. 'He knows me personally.'

'We don't care,' shouted the guards, blocking their way with spears. 'We have strict orders that Raja Tejbali is not to be disturbed under any circumstances.'

'Now what do we do?' whispered Anindita.

Arjun took a few steps forward and fixed the guards with a steely gaze. 'We've been sent by Shwetvardhan to deliver an important message to Raja Tejbali. You shall answer to the Mahanagri Parishad if you don't let us through.'

The guards squirmed uncomfortably. Should they let the children through? But what would the king say? On the other hand, they had no authority to stop messengers from the Mahanagri Parishad. They finally moved aside.

One of the guards accompanied Arjun and Anindita to the king's chamber, where he was in an intense discussion with Lohadil about the positioning of the toy tanks along the border.

'Come in,' Raja Tejbali's voice rang from inside.

The guard pushed open the door, but Lohadil almost pounced upon him before he could utter a single word. 'Don't you see we're busy here?' he barked. 'How dare you ...'

'Calm down,' sighed the king, ushering the guard inside. 'What do you want?'

'My sincere apologies for disturbing you, Maharaj,' replied the guard, bowing deeply, even as Lohadil eyed them with suspicion, 'but these children from Manav Lok say they've been sent by Shwetvardhan, the respected elder.'

'We seek forgiveness for the intrusion, Maharaj,' said Arjun, as the king dismissed the guard. 'Actually, we haven't been sent by Shwetvardhan, although we do know him well. The reason we're here is to see if we can help prevent this war in any way.'

'Please don't send all those poor toys to war,' pleaded Anindita, her eyes brimming with tears.

Lohadil stomped up to them. 'What utter nonsense is this!' he shouted. He swivelled around and threw his arms up in the air. 'Are we now going to listen to some children about how we should defend our land? We don't have time for this, Maharaj.'

'Some children?' retorted Arjun angrily. 'For your information, we've helped Chamatkar Nagri overcome the likes of Krooradasa and Dushtasura. And we really care about what happens to the toys.'

'I've heard about you,' said Raja Tejbali, his eyes sparking with interest. 'Do you really have suggestions? I wish Shwetvardhan knew about this.'

'You mean you haven't told him about the war?' asked Anindita, as Arjun looked on incredulously. 'You have to tell him. He'll know what to do.'

'I don't think so,' grumbled Lohadil, glaring at the children.

But the King of Khilonapatnam had made up his mind. 'We should have called him earlier,' he said gravely, picking up the receiver of a toy phone with a large screen. He looked up at Arjun and remarked. 'We're the only creatures in Chamatkar Nagri that can't do magic.'

Moments later, Shwetvardhan's face appeared. 'Hello, Tejbali,' he smiled. 'It's nice to hear from you. I hope everything's all right.'

'I'm afraid it isn't,' replied Raja Tejbali. He had soon narrated everything to the senior-most elder of the Mahanagri Parishad.

Shwetvardhan's jaw was set in a hard line by the end of the conversation. 'Why didn't you bring this to my attention earlier?' he thundered. 'Do you know the kind of losses there will be if you go ahead with this war? I'm leaving Tashkot right now. I should be there soon.'

Shwetvardhan made the journey to Khilonapatnam in less than an hour. 'You are true friends of Chamatkar Nagri,' he said to the children. He spun around and faced Khilonapatnam's army chief. 'You will not utter another word until all of this is over.'

'Can you please tell us something more about these kripa-kathors?' asked Anindita.

Shwetvardhan nodded at Raja Tejbali.

'As you already know, the kripa-kathors live in Kathorikripa, which neighbours us. They're very gentle when they're in their kripa form, like sheep from Manav Lok. All they do is eat during the day and sleep at night. But when they turn into kathors, their bodies become hard and emaciated and long fangs grow out of their mouths.'

'And you don't want to have anything to do with the kathors,' added Shwetvardhan, with a grim shake of his head.

'They can turn from one form to the other at will. However, they usually turn into kathors only when they're deprived of food.'

Anindita shivered, picturing a cute sheep-like creature turning into a vicious monster.

'As you can imagine, someone stealing their food is a very grave matter,' said Shwetvardhan.

'Isn't there anything we can do?' asked Arjun. He could not imagine the puny toys going against the mighty kathors.

'There is,' replied the senior elder. 'Raja Dayadrohi of Kathorikripa is a good friend. I shall have a word with him right away.'

Arjun squeezed Anindita's hand as Shwetvardhan stepped out to converse with the King of Kathorikripa. But when he returned, it was apparent that things hadn't gone quite as expected. 'It's much more serious than we imagined,' he said, slipping the crystal ball inside his flowing robes. 'Entire fields have vanished within hours. And although Raja Dayadrohi feels that Khilonapatnam isn't responsible, the kripa-kathors are in no mood to listen to him unless he can present them with evidence.'

Arjun leaned upon the map. 'Are there any other lands that border Kathorikripa?'

'Yes, they share a border with Paschimi Ilaka as well,' replied Raja Tejbali.

'So why are the kripa-kathors so sure that Khilonapatnam is responsible for the theft?'

'Because the inhabitants of Paschimi Ilaka eat from the swamps. Why would they steal food from the kripa-kathors?'

'What if it's not about the food at all?' said Arjun. He straightened up and looked at the others intently. 'What if Paschimi Ilaka is playing a bigger game? What if they're trying to frame Khilonapatnam?'

Shwetvardhan ran his fingers through his beard. 'I think you're absolutely right,' he said, bobbing his head gently. 'Why do you think I was in Tashkot? I had been asked to investigate reports that the vetalas—evil shape-shifters—were trying to foment trouble in Chamatkar Nagri. And where do you think these vetalas live?'

'Right across the Kathorikripa border in Paschimi Ilaka,' interjected Lohadil, emerging from hibernation. 'We must inform the kripa-kathors immediately.'

'Don't be hasty,' said Shwetvardhan. 'It remains a theory until we can offer solid proof to the kripa-kathors.'

Raja Tejbali wrung his arms in despair. 'But why would the vetalas want to frame us?' he asked, agitatedly.

The senior elder stared out of the window, lost in the glow of the street lamps for a few moments. 'The vetalas have opposed the peace treaty between our lands for a very long time,' he replied, turning around with a sigh. 'So far, they've made several unsuccessful attempts on Tashkot, the only land in Chamatkar Nagri to share a border with Paschimi Ilaka. However, it seems like they've adopted a very different tactic this time. If war were to break out between Kathorikripa and Khilonapatnam, it would weaken both the lands and allow the vetalas to move in swiftly. If we can't stop this war, it will only be a matter of time before they overrun the rest of Chamatkar Nagri. We must thwart their evil plans.'

'But how? The kripa-kathors will launch an attack anytime now.'

'Did you say that entire fields have vanished within hours?' asked Arjun, sitting up straight.

'That's what Raja Dayadrohi mentioned,' replied Shwetvardhan.

Arjun pressed his fingers tightly against each other, pausing to think. 'Okay,' he said, taking a deep breath. 'There's no way the toys could have done it. They can't do magic. So how can they make fields disappear from Kathorikripa? It is obvious that the vetalas are behind this.'

'Of course,' said Raja Tejbali animatedly. 'Shwetvardhan, you must inform their king immediately.'

But Arjun shook his head. 'The idea is to not only prove the innocence of the toys but also provide concrete evidence about the involvement of the vetalas.'

Shwetvardhan looked at him with keen eyes. 'Something tells me you have a plan.'

'Chamatkar Nagri has a peace treaty with Kathorikripa. Even their king believes that the toys aren't involved. And yet, the kripa-kathors have been inclined to go to war with Khilonapatnam.'

'You're absolutely right.'

'And just now, you said the vetalas are shape-shifters. It is very likely that a few of them have assumed the form of the kripa-kathors to instigate trouble.'

'It's plausible. But how can we expose the imposters? The kripa-kathors are born from seeds. So they don't have family. And since they only care about eating, they don't really know each other. If somebody is posing as a kripa-kathor, it would be near impossible to identify the culprit.'

'What can we do?' wailed Anindita. 'I really don't want the kripas to turn into their monstrous kathor forms.'

Arjun gave a low whistle. 'You've given me an idea, Anu!' he said, turning to Shwetvardhan. 'The imposters have obviously turned themselves into kripas. But can they transform from kripas to kathors directly?'

Shwetvardhan smiled. 'They would have to turn into their original vetala forms before they can do that. Brilliant, Arjun! I shall have a word with Raja Dayadrohi immediately.'

Peace soon returned to Khilonapatnam. It hadn't taken long for the kripa-kathors to detect the imposters. As suspected, the vetalas from Paschimi Ilaka had infiltrated the kripa-kathor population. They had used magic to make the food disappear. And while the kripa-kathors had been busy amassing their army along the border with Khilonapatnam, they had made plans to launch an attack.

Shwetvardhan walked in. 'I have just received word that the vetalas have fled from the borders of Kathorikripa. We've also dispatched some elders to restore the fields that have disappeared.'

Raja Tejbali wiped his brow. 'It was a very close call indeed. But we're safe now.'

'And we owe it all to Arjun,' Shwetvardhan added.

'Actually, we wouldn't have been here had Anindita not insisted,' said Arjun, putting an arm around his sister.

Soon, their toys were ushered inside the palace.

'You're both heroes of Khilonapatnam,' said Lohadil, who had also admitted that a war would have been catastrophic.

'And we would like to honour you for your invaluable service,' said Raja Tejbali. 'Please step forward.'

Loud cheers echoed all around as the King of Khilonapatnam pinned a shiny button on Anindita's dress. Arjun got one as well.

The ceremony was followed by grand celebrations that went on until the wee hours of the morning. But it was soon time to leave. As everyone watched in amazement, Shwetvardhan transformed their toy plane into a real one, and before long, the children and their toys were flying through the clear skies towards Manav Lok.

They woke up in their bed to a bright and sunny morning. Anindita rushed to her dolls. They were lifeless once again, but Radha was clutching a tiny piece of paper. It read:

CHATURANG'S CAR

'I can't understand why this Petumal would kidnap Mishti,' said Shilpjeet, the curator of the newly opened Chamatkar Nagri museum. 'She's just a harmless pari.'

He was sitting in the Jaduprastha police station with Dandagupt, the chief of police. Dandagupt was staring at the piece of paper that had been left in the room that housed the inventions. It simply read:

> I have the pari.
> Wait for furthur instructions.
>
> signed Jadugar Petumal

'So what does this Mishti do?' asked the police chief.

'She's the caretaker of the museum.'

'I see. Was anything stolen?'

'That's the strange part. The museum has many valuable things, but nothing was taken.'

'It would appear that this Petumal had come for something specific but when he didn't find it, he took the pari instead.'

Just then, Nyayadoot, Dandagupt's deputy, walked in. 'There's not much information about Petumal,' he said. 'All we know is that he recently bought an island in Krodha Sagar, off the south-western coast of Chamatkar Nagri. He lives there alone in a fortress called Manthan Gadh.'

'Pardon me, sir, but a large black crow just dropped this at the museum,' said a frightened pari, carrying a piece of paper.

'This is my assistant, Rish,' said Shilpjeet, taking the paper from the pari's outstretched fingers. His expression turned to one of surprise.

'What does it say?' asked Dandagupt.

'Petumal wants Jadugar Chaturang's enchanted car within 24 hours. Otherwise, he has threatened to send Mishti to Patala.'

'What does this car do exactly? Is it an important invention?'

'Not at all. It's just a car that can fly. It was invented by Jadugar Chaturang over 50 years ago.'

'Why would anyone steal a car that flies when there are carpets available?' asked Nyayadoot. 'Anyway, let's just give him this car and get Mishti back.'

But Shilpjeet shook his head. 'That's not possible since we don't have it in the first place.'

'What do you mean you don't have it?' asked Dandagupt in an irritated voice. He pushed a copy of the previous day's edition of *Indrajaal*, Chamatkar Nagri's leading newspaper. 'The car's pictures have been splashed all over the front page.'

'You were fooled just as Petumal was,' sighed Shilpjeet. 'That picture is from an old photo. The museum display is actually a very good replica of the car. Petumal obviously realized this and decided to take Mishti instead.'

'Then we must get in touch with Jadugar Chaturang.'

'I'm afraid that won't be possible either. Jadugar Chaturang disappeared 50 years ago, soon after he built that car. Some say he defected to Paschimi Ilaka, while others are convinced he crossed into Patala. There was also a rumour that he had travelled to Manav Lok.'

'So what do we do now?' asked Dandagupt, sinking into his chair with a loud sigh.

Meanwhile, in Manav Lok ...

Arjun and Anindita were playing catch when their ball bounced inside Robert Chacha's auto-repair shop. Anindita followed it as it rolled under a car standing in a dimly lit corner of the shop.

'Arjun, look at this,' said Anindita, lifting one of the many plastic sheets that covered the car. She covered her mouth as the dust flew all over.

'That's a fancy car,' said Arjun, running over. And indeed it was. The long, sleek looking car was bright red in colour, with silver edges and no roof. The seats, upholstered with rich black leather, were faded and creased. The front had two almond-shaped headlights and tapered into a silver grill that had dulled over time. But the strangest part was that it did not have a steering wheel.

'I see you've found the funny car,' said Robert Chacha, walking over. He wiped his hands on his soiled overalls and smiled. 'Although it still looks quite nice, this car has been sitting in our garage since I was a child. My father told me that a man dressed in strange robes dropped it here one dark, rainy night and never returned to pick it up. I suppose it's been about 50 years since this happened.'

'Can we play in it, Robert Chacha?' asked Anindita.

'If you can move it from here, you can keep it,' said Robert Chacha, laughing. 'It's been blocking my space all these years.'

'Is there anyone who can help me?' a customer's voice floated in from the counter. Robert Chacha excused himself and ran outside.

'How could anyone have driven this car without a steering wheel?' wondered Arjun, staring at the empty dashboard. He opened the door and bent down to see if there was any mechanism to make the car move. As he leaned forward, a coin fell from inside his pocket and slipped under the seat. Arjun slid his hand under the seat to feel around for the coin, but it was no use. As he was pulling his hand out, his fingers brushed against something soft. Arjun quickly pulled out the object.

'Open it, open it,' cried Anindita excitedly, looking at the red satin pouch in Arjun's hand.

Arjun loosened the silver string and peered inside to find a small piece of paper, yellowed with age. The writing on the page wasn't legible in the dim light.

Suddenly, Anindita remembered that they had to be home for an early dinner, since Dada and Dadi had to go out. Arjun pushed the paper inside his pocket with a reluctant nod. They waved goodbye to Robert Chacha and started back.

Shortly before midnight, Arjun suddenly remembered the piece of paper in his pocket. Flattening the paper under the table lamp, he slowly read out the faded text.

If you want to fly and know the place
Just say its name, I'm ready to race
If you want to fly and don't know where
Just follow my lead, I'll take you there

'Arjun, the car is enchanted,' shouted Anindita, clapping her hands in joy.

Arjun ran around her with his arms outstretched. 'We're going to fly, we're going to fly.'

'We must go to Robert Chacha's garage first thing tomorrow morning.'

'But where should we take the car? There are so many places I've always wanted to visit.'

'This is so exciting. I don't think I can sleep tonight.'

Before Arjun could reply, the air was filled with the honking of a car horn.

'What's that noise? Have Dada-Dadi returned?'

Anindita ran over to the window and drew the curtains aside. There, in front of her, was the car from Robert Chacha's garage, hovering outside the window. It was flashing its almond-shaped headlights and honking impatiently.

'I ... I think it wants us to get inside,' whispered Anindita, nudging her brother. 'It must have flown here after you read the spell. Doesn't it look pretty?'

The car did indeed look magnificent under the indigo skies. The ethereal moonlight bounced off its silver edges, giving it a sophisticated look that made their hearts miss a beat. But what amazed them the most were the two beautiful wings with cascading silver feathers that were flapping mightily on either side. The car slowly descended towards the window and opened its door with a quick inviting honk. The children hopped in without a moment's hesitation.

'Do you know where we're going?' asked Anindita in a worried voice as the car rose up in the air.

Arjun shook his head. 'But don't you remember what the writing said? I'm quite sure the car knows where it's taking us.'

Before Anindita could reply, the car soared into the skies. Soon, they were zipping through the faintly illuminated clouds, the cold wind rushing against their faces. When the car suddenly dipped and plunged through the cloud cover a few hours later, they saw a beautiful place set in the midst of mist covered mountains. Flowers of every colour and hue—red, orange, violet and more—bloomed on the lush green mounds, and strange-looking houses in earthy shades stood along winding cobbled paths. Gentle streams with charming stone bridges flowed through the plains. The sight left Arjun and Anindita spellbound.

A large crowd of paris gathered around as the car landed with a few gentle bumps and withdrew its wings. The sound of their chattering brought Nyayadoot out of the police station. 'What's going on here?' his voice boomed.

'This car just flew into Jaduprastha,' replied a pari. 'And it's carrying two children from Manav Lok.'

'Jadugar Chaturang's enchanted car,' exclaimed Nyayadoot, making his way through. 'Why, we were just talking about it a couple of hours ago. How in the world did you come into its possession?'

'We found it in a garage near where we stay,' replied Anindita. 'It had been lying there for 50 years. My brother read a spell, and it brought us here.'

'Then you must come and have a word with our police chief.'

Dandagupt was taken aback at the sight of his deputy leading two children from Manav Lok into the police station.

'Chief, you're not going to believe this,' said Nyayadoot, 'but these children just landed outside in the enchanted car.'

'What?' cried Dandagupt, jumping out of his seat. 'There's no time to waste. Please call the curator of the Chamatkar Nagri museum right away.'

As Nyayadoot rushed out, the police chief of Jaduprastha explained how Jadugar Petumal had kidnapped Mishti and threatened to send her to Patala, if the enchanted car was not handed over to him. Just then, Shilpjeet and Nyayadoot walked in.

'Poor, poor Mishti,' said Anindita. 'We must save her.'

'But why does this Jadugar Petumal want the car?' asked Arjun.

'That's something we don't know,' replied Shilpjeet.

'Nyayadoot mentioned that this car was made by Jadugar Chaturang. What do we know about him?'

'Well, Chaturang was a great jadugar who was accused of stealing some very powerful spells from Jaduprastha's vault of magic about 50 years ago. He disappeared a few days later and hasn't been seen since.'

Anindita thought for a moment. 'We definitely know he visited Manav Lok,' she said. 'Arjun, remember the man in strange robes that Robert Chacha mentioned? The one who dropped the car off at his garage? He must have been Jadugar Chaturang.'

'It had to have been him,' nodded Dandagupt. 'I wonder what happened to all the spells that were stolen though.'

'They're in the car,' said Arjun, biting his lower lip. 'They must be. Think about it. Why would Petumal go through all this trouble to get a flying car when there are so many other things he could use to fly? He's not after the car but something that's inside it.'

'So ... is it possible that this Petumal is none other than Jadugar Chaturang?' asked Nyayadoot.

Arjun shook his head. 'Not likely,' he replied. 'If Jadugar Chaturang had stolen the spells and hidden them inside the car, he would never have left it in Manav Lok and gone away.'

'Then how did Petumal know about the location of the spells?' asked Shilpjeet in a perplexed voice.

'It's very simple. He must either be the person who stole the spells or is someone who knows the thief well. It's very possible he had some connection with Jadugar Chaturang and framed him. Is there any way to find out?'

'Jadgugar Chaturang didn't have any family or friends,' replied Shilpjeet. 'He was dedicated to his work. But he did have an assistant, a yaksha named Lalchi.'

Arjun brought his palms together and closed his eyes. 'It's very likely that this Lalchi is now posing as Petumal,' he said. 'He must have stolen the spells and planted evidence against his master before hiding them in the enchanted car. But, before he could get to them, Jadugar Chaturang must have used the same car to escape to Manav Lok. Petumal obviously had no idea where the car was until its picture appeared in the newspaper. By the way, what were those spells for?'

'Since they were top secret, it was never revealed,' replied Shilpjeet.

'The first thing we need to do is find those spells,' said Dandagupt.

Soon, they were all searching the car for the stolen spells. An hour later, Nyayadoot found them hidden inside the left headlight.

'I must take them back to the vault immediately,' said Dandagupt.

'But what about poor Mishti?' asked Anindita in alarm.

'Chief Dandagupt is right,' said Arjun. 'We can't let the spells fall into the hands of that evil Petumal under any circumstances.' Before his sister could protest, he continued, 'I do have a plan to rescue the pari, though. Shilpjeet and I will take the car to Petumal. He has no idea that we know about the stolen spells. So when we hand it over, he will think they're all still hidden inside. Meanwhile, we shall take Mishti and be on our way.'

'But Petumal stays on an island in the middle of Krodha Sagar,' said Nyayadoot. 'How will you escape without the car?'

'I still have to figure out that bit,' confessed Arjun, blowing into his hands. 'But there's no time to lose. We'll think of something along the way.'

'I'm coming with you,' said Anindita, jumping inside the car.

Arjun started to object but then stopped and gave a gentle nod instead. He knew how adamant his sister could be. 'Manthan Gadh,' he said, wondering what dangers lay ahead.

The car passed over many lands—some new, others vaguely familiar—until it finally reached the south-western border of Chamatkar Nagri, beyond which stretched the mighty Krodha Sagar. A few miles later, they encountered tall thunderous waves that rose high in the air and sent out a spray of water that made their car shake violently. Arjun and Anindita held on tight, fear clouding their sweat-drenched faces.

'Higher,' shouted Arjun, wiping his cheeks against his sleeve. He fell back

with a sigh of relief as the car powered through the clouds.

The remaining part of their journey was largely uneventful. They finally descended upon the island – a small piece of barren land surrounded by sharp black cliffs that were under the constant onslaught of waves. Manthan Gadh, built out of large blocks of coarse, grey stone, stood in a dilapidated state on one side. All of a sudden, it shook, sending rubble cascading down its sides.

'No wonder it's called Manthan Gadh,' chuckled Shilpjeet.

A burly yaksha with a thick jaw and bald head, and wearing a long robe and a tall hat to give the appearance of a jadugar, waited impatiently on top of the fortress. It was none other than Petumal. The gold ring in his nose shone wickedly as his head followed the trajectory of the car until it landed in a small clearing nearby.

'The enchanted car,' croaked Petumal, his voice trembling with emotion. 'I have waited 50 long years for this day.'

'Where's Mishti?' asked Arjun.

The rogue yaksha glared back. 'Such impudence,' he barked. 'Do you think I want to keep that wretched creature here for another second? She's been howling the entire time. Bhondu, bring the pari.'

'How do we leave this place?' asked Arjun, a little hesitantly. It was quite apparent that the yaksha didn't want them there. Perhaps he would provide them with the means to leave.

Petumal, who had been admiring the car, looked up in disgust. 'Give them some brooms and throw them out. I have important work to do.'

Much to Arjun's delight, Bhondu led them up the round staircase along with the pari and the brooms. They had what they needed. His plan had worked. But they would have to hurry.

Unfortunately, things were about to get ugly. 'Halt!' Petumal's voice thundered through the tower like an avalanche and was followed by the sound of his footsteps as he rushed towards them. Bhondu, who had sensed that something was wrong, blocked the way down. They were trapped.

'What do we do?' squeaked Anindita, as Mishti clung tightly to her side.

'So you thought you could fool me, did you?' screamed Petumal. 'Fifty years. That's how much time I've spent in Patala. Yes, I was banished there by that fool, Chaturang. But I won't wait any longer. Where are my magic spells?'

'In their rightful place inside the Jaduprastha vault of magic,' shouted Arjun.

Petumal went red in the face. 'Then you're all my hostages. And if they don't give me what I want, I shall turn you all into toadstools.'

Arjun could feel the hair on his neck stand on end. Shilpjeet froze in his tracks, and Mishti and Anindita burst into tears. Things were beginning to look quite bleak. And just as Arjun thought that everything was lost, he was struck by an idea. He quickly chanted the car spell under his breath. He would now have to distract Petumal. 'Jadugar Chaturang will banish you to Patala once again,' he shouted, as defiantly as he could.

Arjun thought that his words would provoke Petumal to give a verbal response. Unfortunately, they had the opposite effect. The yaksha drew out his wand, seething with fury.

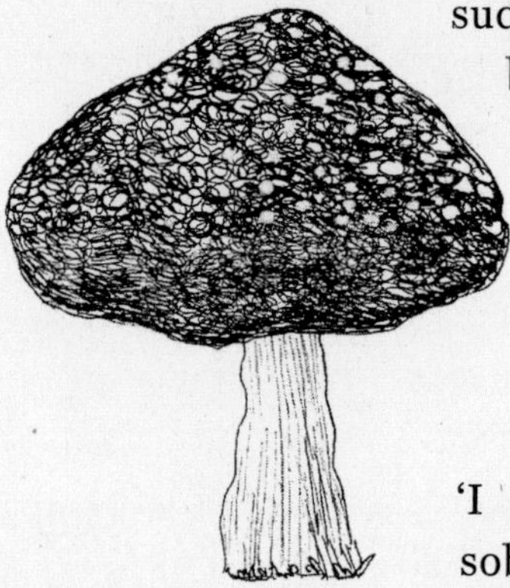

Arjun had almost given up any hope of escaping alive, when suddenly, the fortress gave a shudder, throwing Petumal off balance. The spell that shot out of his wand completely missed its mark and struck poor Bhondu instead. Almost instantly, a mouldy green toadstool stood in his place.

The very next moment, the car appeared outside the window and honked. 'Everyone inside, now,' cried Arjun, pushing the others out. 'Jaduprastha!'

'I can't believe we escaped from that horrible place,' sobbed Anindita as the car took off towards the capital of Chamatkar Nagri.

'We're not out of it yet,' shouted Shilpjeet as the waves of Krodha Sagar raged below. 'Petumal is right behind us. And I'm afraid he'll catch up with us as his broom is faster than the car.'

They spotted a speck in the distance that grew larger every second. Petumal was covering the distance swiftly and, despite the noise, could be heard hurling curses at them.

'What can we do?' said Arjun, looking at the others despondently. 'I'm not sure how we're going to get out of this one. He's just too fast.'

'He's drawing his wand,' groaned Shilpjeet, as the yaksha drew nearer.

'Car, please help us escape,' begged Anindita.

The car honked loudly, sending out a big burst of thick black smoke right into Petumal's face.

'My eyes, my eyes,' screeched the evil yaksha, as he was struck by a bad coughing fit. He lost control of his broom and plunged into the tumultuous waves of Krodha Sagar below.

Mishti hugged Arjun and Anindita the moment they all landed in

Jaduprastha. 'It was so cold and scary inside that fortress, and it kept shaking!' she told Anindita between sobs.

While the children had been away on the rescue mission, Jadugar Chaturang had returned to Chamatkar Nagri. He had been granted official pardon by the Mahanagri Parishad and exonerated of all charges. 'I owe you a debt of gratitude for clearing my name, children,' he said, clasping their hands warmly.

'I was wondering,' Arjun said, 'why did you disappear from Chamatkar Nagri?'

'It probably wasn't the right course of action, but I didn't have a choice. I knew that Lalchi, or Petumal as you know him, had stolen the spells. I even tried to coax him, cajole him into telling me where he had hidden them, but he wouldn't. So I finally banished him to Patala. It's possible someone might have seen me and assumed that I was crossing over. Unfortunately, Lalchi planted false evidence inside the vault to frame me. I couldn't go to the police without any proof. So I left for Manav Lok in the car and lived inside a cave all these years. And to think the spells had been right under my nose.'

'I'm tired,' yawned Anindita, stretching her arms. 'Can you please send us back, Jadugar Chaturang?'

'Well, you don't need my help. You have the car. It's the least I can do.'

Anindita jumped up and down in glee, but Arjun wasn't so sure. 'Where will we keep it?' he asked gloomily.

'Don't worry. I shall give you a spell to shrink it, so you can carry it inside your pocket. Whenever you need to use it, simply say the spell again, and it will grow to its normal size.'

Arjun and Anindita waved to everyone and soared into the skies in their very own enchanted car. But they were too tired to enjoy the ride back and fell asleep almost immediately. When they reached home, the car honked gently. Luckily, Dada-Dadi were still in bed. Arjun shrunk the car and kept it next to Aladdin's lamp. Then the two of them quietly slipped into bed.

The Key of Avatar

'I really wonder if Chamatkar Nagri's peace treaty with the kalpanic pranis is going to be of any use when they can't get along with their own brethren,' sighed Shwetvardhan. 'According to this report, there's trouble brewing between the jal pranis and the bhoomi pranis once again.'

'They do fight over the silliest things,' remarked Gyandarshan. 'I remember the time they couldn't decide who would represent their land in the annual magic conference. We had to finally allow two representatives amidst protests from the other lands.'

'I'm afraid it's a much more serious matter this time. If a solution isn't found soon, the consequences shall be felt not only in Chamatkar Nagri but also in Manav Lok.'

'But what are they fighting about?' asked Bhadradharma.

Shwetvardhan waved his hands over the crystal ball until it fogged up again. 'The jal pranis are demanding that they be given the Key of Avatar.'

'Why do they want this key?' asked Gyandarshan. 'Does it unlock some magical power or something?'

'The Key of Avatar opens gateways into Manav Lok,' replied Bhadradharma. 'However, it can only be used by the kalpanic pranis.'

'The jal pranis want to enter Manav Lok, while the bhoomi pranis are against it,' continued Shwetvardhan. 'If the jal pranis succeed, it will result in a major crisis.'

'This is very unfortunate,' said Gyandarshan.

'A war between the jal pranis and the bhoomi pranis looks inevitable. And it's almost certain that the jal pranis will win, since they're stronger and outnumber their counterparts on land.'

'Isn't there anything we can do?'

'I was coming to that. We have a peace treaty with Kalpanadweep. If we decide to interfere in their internal affairs, it will amount to a violation of the treaty.'

'Perhaps it's wiser to simply wait and watch,' suggested Bhadradharma.

'I don't think we can do that either. If the jal pranis get the Key of Avatar, the harmonious order that exists will be disturbed, leading to considerable upheaval in Chamatkar Nagri, not to mention the chaos that will result in Manav Lok.'

'But what about the peace treaty?' asked Gyandarshan.

Shwetvardhan's face bore a pained look. 'It's not a decision I've taken lightly.'

There was silence.

'What do you propose to do?' asked Bhadradharma.

'I shall offer to act as a mediator.'

'And if that fails?'

'If a war was to break out between the jal pranis and the bhoomi

pranis, we shall be forced to support the bhoomi pranis,' replied Shwetvardhan grimly. 'We have to employ all the resources at our disposal to ensure that the jal pranis remain in Kalpana Mahasagar. If the bhoomi pranis fall, we shall all pay a tremendous price.'

'But if we break the peace treaty, none of the other lands shall ever place their trust in us again,' said Gyandarshan.

'Your concerns are valid,' replied the senior elder gently. 'But that should be the least of our worries since, at the moment, the very survival of Chamatkar Nagri is at stake. However, I shall do everything in my power to avert this disaster.'

Meanwhile, in Manav Lok ...

'This looks like the perfect spot,' said Anindita, spreading the cloth on a grassy patch under the shade of a large tree. The serene waters of a pond nearby glistened under the morning sun.

It was a glorious day, and Dadi had insisted that the children have a picnic in the woods. She had packed a basket of delicious goodies, aloo tikkis, cheese theplas, masala samosas, peas and paneer sandwiches, beetroot hummus with papdi, date biscuits, mawa cake and a large flask of ginger lemonade.

'It was a great idea to have a picnic today,' said Arjun, turning his face upwards. Warm sunshine trickled in through the rustling leaves. 'I must say, I'm beginning to enjoy the village.'

'Are you sure you don't mean Chamatkar Nagri?' teased Anindita, opening the basket. She let her nose hover above it for a few moments. 'Everything smells so delicious. Shall we eat?'

But Arjun ran over to the pond. 'Let's sail a few boats first.'

'Why don't you start while I set the food?'

As Arjun crafted the paper boats, Anindita began to unpack the basket.

'Are you Arjun?' said a tiny voice from behind just as he was about to set the first boat adrift. Arjun turned around to see a stout pari making his way towards him through the blades of grass. 'I'm so relieved to have found you,' continued the pari after receiving a nod. 'I'm Bir. I've been sent by Shwetvardhan, the respected elder, to inform you that Manav Lok may be in trouble. He has requested that you accompany me.'

Arjun called out to his sister. Anindita came running, as surprised as her brother.

'Shwetvardhan's called us,' said Arjun. 'We have to leave for Chamatkar Nagri immediately.'

'Not Chamatkar Nagri,' corrected Bir. 'We shall be heading to Kalapanadweep.'

'But how do we get there? Should we go get the enchanted car? Or should we search for the door?'

'The door's been sick for the past few days, and we don't have time to go back to your house. But this paper boat will do nicely.'

Arjun and Anindita looked at each other in surprise as Bir drew a circle on the muddy patch by the pond. Chamatkar Nagri never ceased to amaze them.

'Step inside, please,' instructed the pari, hopping in. As he muttered a spell, everything around them started to grow larger. While Arjun had experienced a shrinking spell before, it was all new for Anindita. They pushed the paper boat towards the edge. Arjun and Anindita climbed inside carefully, making sure it didn't topple over. Bir pushed the boat and quickly jumped in as it floated out into the water. He then removed a wand and chanted out aloud while tapping the edge of the boat.

'Oh, little paper boat in the pond,
Heed the command of my wand.
As soon as I tap you times three,
Set us afloat in the mythical sea.'

The next moment a blistering wind blew in through the woods, crashing against the surface and sending a spray of water at them. When Arjun and Anindita opened their eyes, they weren't in the paper boat anymore. Instead, they found themselves on a wooden ship, surrounded by choppy waves as far as the eye could see.

Bir waved at them as he steered the ship. 'We're in Kalpana Mahasagar,' he shouted over the noise of the waves. 'It's all a part of Kalpanadweep. We should be reaching the land mass soon, where Shwetvardhan, the respected elder, awaits us.'

It wasn't long before they reached an exotic island with golden shores and lush vegetation, surrounded by azure waters. The only visible structure was a tower that rose into the sky on the other side of the island. Bir guided the ship into a small cove, where Shwetvardhan stood with an uncharacteristically impatient look. 'I'm glad you could make it at such short notice, children,' he said, helping Anindita out of the ship. 'A grave threat looms over both

Chamatkar Nagri and Manav Lok.'

Arjun could feel his heart in his mouth as the senior elder directed them towards a small wooden hut on the beach. What could this threat be, he wondered.

'Our story begins almost five hundred years ago when Kalapanadweep was ruled by Raja Avatar,' began Shwetvardhan. 'He was a rikshaja, a creature that is part goat and part bear. A fair and just king, he ruled wisely for many years. However, towards the end of his reign, parnalas started attacking the pranis. To protect his kind, Raja Avatar sought the help of Raja Prabhavshali, the powerful King of Chamatkar Nagri. Together, they forged a magical key to help the pranis take temporary refuge in Manav Lok to escape the parnala attacks. This came to be known as the Key of Avatar.'

'What are parnalas?' asked Arjun.

'They're brown, humpbacked, winged creatures with horns and fangs and a tail that slithers behind them like a snake.'

Anindita gave a little shudder. 'Do they still exist?'

'About a century ago, Raja Vayumitra—a direct descendent of Raja Avatar—and the Mahanagri Parishad used extremely powerful magic to turn all the parnalas to stone. The key was then sealed inside Akash Minar. Raja Vayumitra divided the pranis into two groups, the jal pranis and the bhoomi pranis, and gave each group a seal. Only when both the seals are joined can the Akash Minar be opened. And now, the jal pranis want the Key of Avatar.'

'But why would they want the key when the threat from the parnalas no longer exists?' asked Arjun.

'Shatrujeet, leader of the jal pranis, claims they don't have enough room in the seas. But Kalpana Mahasagar covers a vast area. It is, in fact, the bhoomi pranis who should be complaining, since they're confined to this piece of land.'

Anindita looked around. 'Where are we exactly?'

'Kalpanadweep lies just beyond the southernmost tip of Chamatkar Nagri.'

Just then, Bir returned with some beverages and snacks.

'What do the bhoomi pranis have to say?' asked Arjun, sipping the clear amber liquid.

'The bhoomi pranis are against opening the gateways into Manav Lok. They feel that someone is instigating the jal pranis. I feel the same.'

Arjun glanced outside the hut at the sweeping expanse of the clear blue waters. 'I'm confused about one thing here,' he said. 'If the jal pranis enter Manav Lok, there could be a lot of trouble there. But why should this cause any problems in Chamatkar Nagri?'

'Well, if the gateways to Manav Lok are opened, the spell that turned the parnalas to stone will break, and they will return to life. If that were to happen, we shall once again be thrust into the dark ages.'

'So why don't you stop the jal pranis?' asked Anindita innocently.

'I really wish it were that easy. There's a peace treaty between Kalpanadweep and Chamatkar Nagri that prevents us from interfering in their internal matters. However, the Mahanagri Parishad has taken a decision to support the bhoomi pranis in case war breaks out. What's worrying is that the jal pranis would have surely figured this out. And since they don't seem to be perturbed in any way, the only conclusion I can draw is that they're being backed by some other power.'

Anindita sat up. 'I just thought of something,' she said. 'We keep hearing stories back home about creatures such as the Loch Ness Monster and the Yeti. Are these actually kalpanic pranis?'

'They're probably descendants of the pranis that got left behind in the past. And since the gateways are now closed, they can no longer return to Kalpanadweep.'

'So what do we do next?' sighed Arjun, pushing his hands behind his head. The situation was looking very grim indeed.

'We should head to Akash Minar. I've scheduled a joint meeting with the bhoomi pranis and the jal pranis there in some time.'

Akash Minar was similar to Suvarna Minar in Chamatkar Nagri, only smaller. Carved out of a single piece of rock, it now lay in ruins, thick vines running all the way to the top. The grooves for the two seals were barely visible under all the growth.

'While the key was placed inside only a hundred years ago, the tower is much older,' said Shwetvardhan.

Arjun parted the vines to take a closer look. As he leaned forward, he noticed some carvings under the grooves. 'There's some writing here,' he shouted, running his palms over it to clean out the dirt. 'I need something sharp to cut these vines.'

A few minutes later, the vines had been cleared to reveal the writing on the tower. Shwetvardhan read it aloud.

WHEN THE TWO ARE UNITED; THE PATH WILL BE LIGHTED
IF YOU DISAGREE WITH YOUR KIN; DON'T BRING THE OUTSIDER IN
IF YOU DO, THERE'S A PRICE TO PAY; OR WORK TOGETHER TO FIND A WAY
WITHIN, YOU WILL FIND THE KEY; THE MEANS TO UNLOCK YOUR DESTINY

As they were trying to figure out these words, a breathless Bir came running up to them. 'Bhadradharma has sent a message that the jal pranis are in contact with Jadugarni Ghrunadasi.'

Before any of them could react, the sea began to froth violently. The turbulent waters parted and the head of a giant serpent wearing a large golden crown emerged. It was Shatrujeet, leader of the jal pranis. He was covered in blue scales that gleamed menacingly under the fierce glow of the afternoon sun. But it was the sharp, towering barbs running all the way down the back of his long, slithery neck that had the children worried. The sea continued to churn as the other jal pranis began to surface from the water behind their leader.

Just then, the island began to shake as the bhoomi pranis, led by Dharamveer, their leader, appeared out of the thicket. Dharamveer, a majestic mahisasimha, had the head of a lion and the body of a bull and was covered in golden fur. He wielded a variety of vicious weapons in his 10 arms. He was mounted upon

a tittiri—a massive bird with a beak that could break through stone—and wings that spanned at least 30 feet. A multitude of ferocious bhoomi pranis followed him.

Arjun and Anindita couldn't help feeling scared in the presence of these terrifying creatures.

'We're honoured by your presence, Shwetvardhan,' said Shatrujeet, with a deep bow.

'These are my friends from Manav Lok, Arjun and Anindita,' said Shwetvardhan. 'They have been of immense assistance to us in the past.'

Both the kings nodded at the children. Anindita smiled shyly while Arjun, a little distracted, managed an awkward bow.

'In fact, Arjun has just found this writing on Akash Minar,' continued the senior elder. He read it out so that it was clearly audible to everyone.

Shatrujeet immediately twisted his head to consult with a black, nine-headed serpent who seemed to be his second-in-command. A few minutes later, he turned around with a smile. 'It's quite apparent from this message that the time has come to retrieve the Key of Avatar.'

'And how did you arrive at this conclusion?' asked Dharamveer, without displaying any emotion.

'I'm happy to explain, one line at a time. When the two are united; the path will be lighted. This means that when the two seals are joined, the gateways to Manav Lok will open. If you disagree with your kin; don't bring the outsider in. This means that if we have a disagreement, as is the case right now, we shouldn't bring any outsiders into the equation. If you do, there's a price to pay; or work together to find a way. This means that if you do bring anyone in, such as Shwetvardhan, it could lead to war. However, if you join us in this quest, we can all find a way together to Manav Lok. Within, you will find the key; the means to unlock your destiny. This means that we shall find the key inside Akash Minar, which will lead us to a glorious future.'

The mahisasimha glared at his counterpart. 'A very convenient interpretation, don't you think?'

'Have you thought about the consequences of opening the gateways,

Shatrujeet?' asked Shwetvardhan. 'There will be mayhem in Chamatkar Nagri if the parnalas are returned to life. Have you forgotten the travails our ancestors went through to turn them all to stone?'

'And what about Manav Lok?' cried Anindita, surprising herself.

Arjun, however, remained quiet, simply observing the exchange.

Shatrujeet pushed his head out further into the skies defiantly. 'We don't care,' he hissed. 'We refuse to remain confined to Kalapana Mahasagar any longer. In Manav Lok, large bodies of water await us to roam around in freely.'

'And what about us?' asked Dharamveer bitterly. 'We're your brothers, living in a much smaller place. Yet, we don't complain.'

'Then join us, brother. That's what the inscription says. We shall take over Manav Lok together. You shall have more land than you've ever dreamt of.'

The mahisasimha drew in his breath and shook his head. 'No, brother,' he replied in a firm voice. 'If it was meant to be, Raja Avatar would have made it possible a very long time ago.'

'We can't remain stuck in the past,' retorted the serpent with a disdainful snort. 'Things have changed now. It's time for the jal pranis to chart a new destiny, with or without you.' Loud cheers erupted in the background.

'But if we open the gateways, we're no better than the parnalas,' pleaded Dharamveer.

'You're weak,' bellowed Shatrujeet, towering above the bhoomi pranis ominously. 'And if it comes to a war, we shall crush you.'

'We have information that you've formed an alliance with Ghrunadasi,' said Shwetvardhan, interrupting the exchange between the kalpanic prani kings.

Shatrujeet coiled his body in until his humongous head loomed in front of the senior elder. 'We don't see the need to discuss our association with anybody in this meeting,' he replied stonily. 'And might I remind you that this remains an internal matter of Kalpanadweep? It would behoove you to remain within your role as a mediator rather than making statements that could be construed as unwanted interference.'

'The Mahanagri Parishad won't take this lying down. We shall do everything in our power to protect Chamatkar Nagri.'

'You do what you have to do,' replied the serpent with an arrogant smile.

Dharamveer walked up to Shwetvardhan. 'We have just received confirmed reports that the jal pranis are being backed by Paschimi Ilaka. There's no choice but to fight.'

'We do have one more option,' said Arjun, who hadn't spoken a single word thus far. 'Give them the Key of Avatar.'

Everybody was surprised, most of all Shatrujeet. 'A wise move indeed,' he smirked, recovering quickly. 'After all, why engage in a meaningless battle when the outcome has already been decided?'

'Listen to me,' said Arjun, facing Shwetvardhan. 'Give them the seal of the bhoomi pranis. I know what I'm doing.'

'Are you absolutely sure about this?' whispered the senior elder. 'The fate of our lands is at stake here.'

Arjun bobbed his head confidently.

Dharamveer was about to object, but Shwetvardhan raised his hand. 'Arjun has helped us out of some very tight situations in the past. He won't let us down.'

'Thank you, brother,' said Shatrujeet, as the mahisasimha handed over the seal of the bhoomi pranis. 'I'm truly happy you agreed to this. We really don't wish any harm upon you, and you're still welcome to join us after we open the gateways.'

The kalpanic pranis from both sides watched with bated breath as the serpent placed the seals inside the grooves. An ominous shadow fell upon the island and the surrounding waters, as heavy, grey-bellied clouds rumbled across the skies. A fierce bolt of blue lightning crashed through the air and struck the ancient tower, splitting it into two. When the dust cleared, a blue rectangular box could be seen lying on a raised platform within the debris.

Shatrujeet pounced upon the box. But what a surprise! There was no key inside. In fact, it was completely empty.

The crisis had passed. The jal pranis were disappointed, even enraged, but there was nothing they could do.

'When the parnalas were turned to stone, the key was no longer required,' explained Arjun.

'But how did you figure out the key wasn't there?' asked Shwetvardhan. Everyone was eager to know, because no one had figured it out.

'Actually, the answer lies in the inscription. Let me explain. When the two are united; the path will be lighted. This means that when the bhoomi pranis and the jal pranis work together, they will be shown the right path. If you disagree with your kin; don't bring the outsider in. This means that if you don't agree on something, stay away from external evil influences. If you do, there's a price to pay; or work together to find a way. This means that if you don't heed the warning, there will be a price to pay – a war in this case. So, it's better to work together and find a solution. Within, you will find the key; the means to unlock your destiny. This means that when you require guidance, the answer doesn't lie anywhere but within yourself. Which means, there isn't any actual key to find.'

The jal pranis realized their folly and apologized to everyone for their shameful conduct. They promised to stay away from any disruptive forces and live in harmony with their brothers. The leaders of the kalpanic pranis bowed before Arjun, who blushed at all the attention.

'Your quick thinking has helped prevent a major tragedy from taking place today,' said Shwetvardhan in a relieved voice.

Anindita ran over and looped her arm around her brother's. 'I'm so proud of you,' she whispered, squeezing his hand.

Arjun smiled at her. 'How about we get back to our picnic then?'

'I see you're eager to return home,' said Shwetvardhan, bringing out his wand. A large wave appeared across the horizon and carried the children away on its crest, amidst loud cheers from the kalpanic pranis. The wave swerved sharply, and before they realized what was happening, they found themselves deposited upon the banks of the pond.

It was picnic time.

Murugan's Map

Exactly 693 years ago in Chamatkar Nagri ...

It was a dark night. A convoy of gandharvas was treading cautiously through Rahasyavan along the northern border of Chamatkar Nagri. They were carrying a large wooden chest filled with Raja Thangaraj's gold mudras to Jaduprastha to deposit in the royal treasury. Karthikeyan—a tall, muscular gandharva—led the way with a lamp, while four others followed, lugging the heavy chest of gold. They were followed by Murugan, the leader, and two gandharva soldiers carrying sharp spears. The lantern cast ghostly shadows on the surrounding trees as the silence of the forest was broken by the crunching sound of their wooden shoes.

'I hope we can leave this forest soon,' whispered one of the chest bearers. 'It feels so eerie and unsafe.'

His companion nodded meekly, casting fearful glances around.

'Hurry up, you two,' hissed Murugan, prodding them from behind. 'There have been sightings of pretas in this area.'

Murugan had been feeling very anxious about the journey through

Rahasyavan. But the other routes would have taken an additional day, and the delivery was an urgent one.

Karthikeyan stopped all of a sudden and raised a hand. Murugan had heard the rustling sounds as well. 'How far?' he whispered.

'A mile,' came the reply.

'How many?'

'At least 30.'

Murugan wiped the beads of sweat from his slender forehead. The pretas would be upon them within the next 10 minutes. It was impossible to run with the chest – if they tried, they would lose the gold mudras and their lives in the process. But something had to be done immediately.

'Seven minutes,' said one of the soldiers.

Murugan quickly brought out a parchment from his coat pocket and unrolled it. He had been carrying it for this very purpose – in case they were attacked along the way. 'Karthikeyan,' he said, urgency resonating in his voice, 'we have to hide the gold immediately. The pretas cannot find it under any circumstances.'

The gandharvas quickly buried the chest, in the light of Karthikeyan's lantern.

'The parchment will act as a map and a guide, and only the person who is in possession of it will be able to find the gold,' said Murugan, bringing out his wand. 'And I've put in several obstacles just in case.'

Only this map can show the gold
Keep it hidden from prying eyes
The clues shall one by one unfold
Forget this place, friends or spies

The moment Murugan finished chanting the spell, all the gandharvas, including him, forgot the location of the gold. The spell had wiped this specific memory from their minds. Only the map could lead them to the chest now. But this wasn't the time to think. The pretas would be upon them within five minutes. They had to run.

And run they did. The pretas gave them chase, but the gandharvas were too fast for them. They reached the border of Rahasyavan and were about to jump into Mantarabad when a powerful gust of wind blew their way from the forest and whisked the map right out of Murugan's fingers. He tried to grab it, but it flew high above the trees. The gandharvas stared in despair as the map flew away and soon disappeared from sight.

Over the next seven centuries, there would be numerous attempts to unearth Raja Thangaraj's gold mudras. But none would be successful.

Present day, Manav Lok ...

'This book about pirates is simply amazing,' remarked Arjun. He glanced at the cover longingly. 'I'm sure there's treasure still lying hidden in remote locations, just waiting to be found.'

'Stop dreaming,' said Anindita, pummelling him with a pillow. 'You and your buried treasure. It's not like we haven't tried to find some in the woods.'

Arjun let his head fall back with a sigh. 'I know,' he said, tossing the book aside. 'But I'm getting bored. Why don't we go out and fly my new kite?'

'That could be fun.'

Arjun grabbed his backpack, and they both headed to the clearing behind their garden. Soon, the blue and purple kite was flying steadily in the open skies.

'It's moving so gracefully,' said Anindita, enthralled by the colourful bits of paper fluttering in its tail.

'Do you want to have a go?' asked Arjun, turning around.

At that very instant, a vicious draught of air grabbed the kite and carried it into the woods. Arjun charged after the kite with Anindita close behind. And then, just as suddenly, the wind died down and the kite dipped through the skies landing in the branches of a tree a few feet away.

'It doesn't look damaged,' said Arjun, straining his neck to get a better look. 'Looks like I'm going to have to climb up. I just hope I can get down again.'

'Please be careful,' said Anindita.

It didn't take Arjun long to reach the kite. However, its tail had to be untangled first. A few minutes of gentle tugging later, he drew it out carefully and let it float down to his sister. It was now time to climb down.

Arjun let his body slide down the trunk as he tried to find a foothold. But just as he was about to grab a branch, his foot slipped. Arjun reached out frantically for something to hold on to, but his hand simply broke through the slender boughs. Anindita screamed from below as her brother dangled in the air. Luckily, one of his arms was still wrapped around the trunk, and he managed to swing his other arm around. Just as Arjun regained his balance, his eye caught the edge of something rolled up and lodged in the branches on the other side. 'Anindita,' he shouted. 'There's something up here. I'm going to knock it down.'

Before Anindita could say anything, a thick yellowed parchment landed with a dull thud by her side.

Arjun slowly made his way down. 'What does it say?' he asked, brushing off the twigs and leaves stuck to his body.

'Nothing. It's empty.'

Arjun took the roll from her. He turned it around and even held it against the sun. Anindita seemed to have been right; there was nothing on it. 'Perhaps you can draw something on it,' he said, tossing it towards her in disappointment.

But just as Anindita caught it, the parchment began to glow. She dropped the thing with a yelp, but Arjun managed to grab it before it hit the ground. A few words had appeared. Arjun read them out:

'You have found me, now hear my say,
Listen well for I'll show you the way.
To a treasure so grand, believe you me,
There's only one chance, one opportunity.
But a fair warning for the faint of heart,
The quest cannot stop once you start.'

'It's ... it's a treasure map,' said Anindita, but her voice was laced with uncertainty. There was a very clear warning in the last two lines.

Arjun, however, was ecstatic. 'Finally,' he said, all pumped up. 'Let's go.'

Before Anindita could reply, the text disappeared and a single line materialized: 'Search the forest where secrets are kept.'

'This is fun,' shouted Arjun gleefully. 'The map's giving us clues to the treasure.'

Even Anindita couldn't help feeling excited. 'What about these woods?' she asked. 'Could this be where the secrets are kept?'

'Perhaps you're right.'

They waited expectantly for the next clue, but when no clue appeared for almost 10 minutes, they began to feel that this might not be the correct place.

'I've got an idea,' said Anindita. 'Let's ask the enchanted car to take us to this forest of secrets.'

'And as luck would have it, it's with me right now,' said Arjun, dangling his backpack.

The car rose above the woods and dashed off towards the mysterious forest. It flew over a completely different part of Chamatkar Nagri, across deep gorges with clear blue streams, across rocky terrains haunted by silent shadows, across mystical valleys straddled by exquisite rainbows, and across mountain peaks capped by pristine snow, until a familiar land wading in a golden blanket of tranquil clouds appeared before them.

'Nidrakhand,' whispered Arjun, as they flew above the land of slumber. It hadn't been that long ago that he had visited the place in search of his sister when she had been kidnapped by Keechad.

Anindita shuddered as she recalled her encounter with Ghrunadasi. She buried her face in her palms and refused to open her eyes until they had crossed into the next land.

And what a bizarre land it was! It looked like the surface of a giant, frothing cauldron. Mysterious robed figures stirred the liquid with long wooden sticks. Bubbles were rising from beneath, dancing to the top before disappearing in a spontaneous burst that released a shower of sparkling magic. And almost instantly, a short gust of wind would blow over, swirl around the twinkling dust and gently urge it into the glass bottles that were floating above. And once the magic was in the bottles, and the cork had popped in, the bottles sprouted wings and flew off. It was Mantarabad, the land of spells.

'Look,' said Anindita, pointing to a vast stretch of trees that had appeared ahead. 'That has to be the forest of secrets.'

The car moved above the sea of green, bumping over the conical tops a few times before somehow squeezing down and adjusting itself in a narrow clearing.

'The forest does seem to be whispering secrets,' said Arjun, shrinking the car and slipping it into his backpack. 'Let's see if the map has another clue for us.'

And sure enough, it did. Another line had appeared below the first one. Anindita read it out: 'Hold your ear close for the next clue.'

'Close to what?' asked Arjun.

'The trees?' replied Anindita with a shrug. 'This is the forest of secrets after all.'

So the two of them pushed their ears against the tall, striated trunks and waited. They could only hear humming sounds at first, but when they listened closely, they realized that the trees were whispering secrets, some recent but most that went back many centuries.

'The treasure lies in a wooden chest; near a cross is its place of rest,' whispered one of the trees all of a sudden.

'We need to find a cross,' said Anindita, pulling her ear away.

'A cross?' said Arjun, casting his gaze around. 'But where do we find a cross in a forest?'

After searching for an hour, they had made no progress. Anindita was about to rest against one of the trunks when she stopped and stared. 'A cross,' she said excitedly, pointing ahead. 'It's a cross.'

And indeed, it was. A couple of the trees ahead had cast shadows that formed a large grey cross on the forest floor. It stood out because the shadows of all the other trees fell in a completely different direction. Just then, a new line appeared on the map: 'At the core, find the willow that wept.'

Arjun scratched his head. 'The core? It must mean the centre of the cross.'

Arjun and Anindita stepped into the intersection of the two shadows and looked around.

'There,' said Anindita, pointing at a tree with a large bouquet of droopy leaves. The next line appeared just as they reached the large willow: 'Fifty paces to the west till the water blue.'

'Sounds quite easy,' said Anindita. 'But how do we know which is west?'

'I don't think we really need to know that,' replied Arjun, staring at a small pond nestled among the trees some distance away, its turquoise blue water carrying the reflection of the surrounding flora. 'Let's go.'

By the time they reached the banks, the next clue had already materialized: 'The rakshasa emerges, 50 years having slept.'

Before Arjun and Anindita could even process the information, the serene waters parted with a thunderous crash and a large monster—over 30 feet tall—emerged. He had only one eye, which sat in the centre of his forehead and wobbled around as it scanned the horizon. The monster thumped his sinewy arms on his enormous chest and let out a deafening roar that sent the water hurtling at the two children, drenching them completely. Anindita shook in fear and began to cry, and even Arjun could feel a wave of fear rise within his chest.

The rakshasa fixed his eye upon them and sang in a hideous voice:

'Dare you disturb rakshasa Paheli?
Now answer me these questions three.
If you succeed, you shall be set free.
Otherwise, devoured like a pea.'

Arjun wiped his face and raised his chin defiantly.

'The more there is of this, the less you see of it,' said Paheli. 'What am I talking about?'

'That's easy,' replied Arjun. 'The answer is darkness.'

The rakshasa punched the water angrily. 'The next one won't be so easy,' he growled, goggling at the children. 'The faster you run, the harder it is to catch. What am I talking about?'

'Your breath. I was expecting something harder.'

Paheli uprooted a tree by the banks and broke it in half over his thigh.

'You may have got that one right as well,' he barked, blowing their hair back, 'but you won't get the next one. The more you take, the more you leave behind. What am I talking about?'

Arjun stared at the rakshasa, but his mind had gone blank. Meanwhile, the rakshasa had already started to rub his stomach in anticipation of his next meal.

Suddenly, Anindita blurted out, 'Footsteps, right? The more steps you take, the more you leave behind.'

'Exactly,' shouted Arjun, jumping up and down. 'The answer is footsteps.'

Paheli's thick moustache drooped at the edges as he cast a gloomy look at the ecstatic children. The waters parted and swallowed him but not before his stomach gave one last unhappy rumble.

'That was a close one,' said Arjun, his knees almost buckling at the thought of how narrowly they had escaped. 'If it hadn't been for your quick thinking, we would have surely ended up in his stomach.'

'I still don't see how two puny children would have satisfied his hunger,' replied Anindita.

Arjun pulled out the map. 'I really hope the next clue isn't as dangerous.'

As expected, another line had appeared: 'The first of the five will provide the glue.'

'The first of five what?' said Arjun, repeating the words in his mind. He finally sat down and pressed his fingers against his brow. But after a few minutes, he shook his head in frustration and flung the paper aside. 'So much time wasted. I should have never stepped out of the house today.'

Anindita picked up the map and stared at it. 'Perhaps we should go over the clues again.'

'You may have something there. Can you please read them all out?'

'Search the forest where secrets are kept.
Hold your ear close for the next clue.
At the core, find the willow that wept.
Fifty paces to the west till the water blue.

The rakshasa emerges, 50 years having slept.
The first of the five will provide the glue.'

'There are five lines above the last clue,' said Arjun. 'So could the first of five mean the first line?'

'Search the forest where secrets are kept? But haven't we been doing that all along?'

Arjun ran his palms down his face. 'We're very close,' he said, chewing on the tip of his thumb. 'I can feel it. But what are we missing?'

'The first something of the five clues will provide the glue.'

'That's it. If we take the first character of each of the five lines and glue them together, we get ...' Arjun took the parchment and glanced down the clues. 'We get the word SHAFT.'

'What does it mean?'

'A shaft is basically a stick. We must search for something that looks like a stick. It will most likely be blended in with the environment to give it a natural appearance.'

The two began to look around, scraping aside the fallen leaves, glancing under the large roots and running their hands around the tree trunks. It was only after half an hour that Anindita finally discovered a wooden stick protruding out of the side of a tree, hidden behind a few branches. She pushed it down as Arjun came running over.

The next moment, the forest floor began to shake, and a large boulder rolled away and crashed into the pond. As it did, an old wooden chest covered in dirt rose from under the ground and a deep voice spoke:

'Lo behold, Raja Thangaraj's gold.
Please return it to its rightful fold.
Murugan's map has had its say,
For Chamatkar Nagri, a grand day.'

'The gold obviously belongs to Chamatkar Nagri,' said Arjun, removing the enchanted car from his backpack. 'Let's give them a surprise.'

'I wonder why it was hidden here in the first place,' said Anindita.

Arjun shrugged as he chanted the spell. But the moment it had returned to its normal size, the car started to honk madly. 'It's trying to warn us,' he said, looking around frantically. 'I think someone's approaching. Help me get this chest inside immediately.'

The children somehow dragged the chest and hauled it inside the car. Just as they jumped in, a group of repugnant creatures with sunken faces and bulging eyes leapt out of the trees and bounded towards them on all fours, revealing their knife-like claws. These were the pretas.

'Jaduprastha!' screamed Anindita, slamming the door.

As the car rose upwards, one of its tyres got caught in the overhanging branches. The pretas leapt into the air, but it cranked up its power and tore through the thicket, leaving behind a trail of broken branches. Unfortunately, a couple of pretas did manage to latch on to the bumper, making the car wobble dangerously. Anindita screamed and clutched the handle tightly as Arjun leaned out and swung his backpack wildly, sending them hurtling down.

'Where did those guys come from?' said Arjun, falling back into his seat. He leaned back and closed his eyes. 'That was another close shave.'

Anindita looked down to ensure that there weren't any other creatures still hanging on. 'I'm still shaking.'

Arjun squeezed her hand. 'Thank you so much, car,' he said, patting its side. 'I can't even imagine what would have happened had you not warned us in time.'

The car honked back as the children sunk into their seats.

'So, you did get to find your treasure finally,' said Anindita, shaking her head with a smile. 'But aren't you sad that you'll have to give up all this gold?'

'For me, it was all about finding the treasure,' replied Arjun. 'I really enjoyed that, although I must say it got really scary towards the end.'

The enchanted car landed outside the Jaduprastha police station and honked loudly.

'This is a pleasant surprise indeed,' said Dandagupt, the chief of police, stepping outside.

'Hello, chief,' grinned Arjun. 'We're sorry to call you out like this, but we couldn't have left all this treasure unguarded, could we?'

'Treasure?' Dandagupt had gone wide-eyed. 'Nyayadoot, please inform the Mahanagri Parishad immediately. As per protocol, we must open the chest only in their presence.'

They were soon joined by a few elders of the Mahanagri Parishad inside the station.

'The fabled gold of Raja Thangaraj,' sighed Shwetvardhan, examining the chest. 'I had never expected this chest to be found. How in the world did you manage to locate something that has remained concealed for almost seven centuries?'

Arjun and Anindita narrated their fantastic adventure as the others listened in rapt attention.

'You were indeed very lucky to escape the pretas. They are merciless thieves that inhabit Patala on the other side of Rahasyavan, quick on their feet and ferocious with their claws. In fact, they were the reason why Raja Thangaraj's gold was lost in the first place.'

It was now the children's turn to be amazed as Shwetvardhan recounted the story of how Murugan's men had escaped the pretas but lost the chest of gold.

'Can we please see the treasure?' asked Anindita.

'Of course,' replied the senior elder, before tapping it with his wand.

The wooden chest sprung open, revealing a large treasure of gold mudras. The glare was so bright that everyone shielded their eyes with the back of their palms.

'This gold is worth a lot,' said Pavitranandan, closing the lid with a loud thud. 'It shall be returned to the descendants of those who lost the gold all those years ago. Murugan's spirit will finally be at peace. Although no one blamed him, the poor gandharva was never the same again.'

'Did you know there's a reward for the return of the gold?' said Shwetvardhan with a smile. He handed five gold mudras each to Arjun and Anindita. 'You deserve it.'

The delighted children thanked the elders and got inside the car.

'We did get our treasure after all,' whispered Arjun, as they soared into the skies above Jaduprastha.

The Makkara Trap

'I don't have a good feeling about this,' said Shwetvardhan. The Mahanagri Parishad had received word that the Makkara had been stolen from Jaduprastha's vault of magic the previous night. The elders were engaged in an emergency meeting in Suvarna Minar.

'Do we know who's responsible?' asked Bhadradharma.

'We have unconfirmed reports that it was a pishacha.'

'But what exactly is this Makkara?' asked Gyandarshan.

'The Makkara was an enchanted book created by Jadugarni Dveshakanta over 200 years ago,' replied Bhadradharma. 'It has four lines inscribed on the first page. Whoever reads these four lines is pulled into the book and trapped inside forever. The spell is so potent that there is no known way of reversing it.'

'Dveshakanta ensnared quite a few of her enemies into the book back in the day,' continued Shwetvardhan, 'until she was defeated by the elders of Chamatkar Nagri. Since then, the Makkara has been locked away inside Jaduprastha's vault of magic. That is, until it was stolen last night.'

A knock on the door interrupted Shwetvardhan. Nyayadoot, the deputy police chief of Jaduprastha, entered. 'We have identified the culprit,' he said, bowing deeply to all the elders. 'It was Keechad, a pishacha, who escaped from

MAKKARA

prison about a year ago. He bribed the yaksha on guard duty with five gold mudras. The yaksha has been jailed, but we have no lead on the whereabouts of the pishacha.'

'Isn't this Keechad the same pishacha who stole the chakora's egg a few weeks ago?' asked Gyandarshan.

Shwetvardhan nodded. 'At the behest of Ghrunadasi,' he replied grimly. 'And that's what worries me. A lowly pishacha shouldn't even know about the Makkara. This all seems to be part of a much bigger conspiracy.'

'So what should we do?' asked Nyayadoot.

'First, warn all the residents of Chamatkar Nagri about the book. And second, issue an alert about Keechad. The sooner we apprehend him, the better.'

'Was anything else taken?' asked Bhadradharma.

'No,' replied Nyayadoot. 'And that's why he was so successful. If the pishacha had asked the yaksha guard to remove a powerful spell, the guard would probably have refused or demanded a much higher bribe. But he thought it was just an ordinary book. There's no doubt that this operation was meticulously planned.'

'This isn't what it seems,' sighed Shwetvardhan. 'There are dark forces at work here. And we can't rest until we find out what exactly is going on.'

Meanwhile, in Manav Lok ...

Arjun was busy putting together the pieces of a jigsaw puzzle Dadi had got for him recently. Anindita was in the living room below, watching her favourite cartoon show on television.

Suddenly, the doorbell rang.

'Anindita, can you please get that?' shouted Dadi from inside the kitchen.

'It's the postman,' said Anindita, opening the door. 'And he's got a package.'

'It must be the science kit Mamma was going to send me,' Arjun yelled excitedly.

'No, it's for me.' Anindita turned the package around, but there wasn't any return address. She quickly tore it open and pulled out the contents. It was a book bound in faded maroon leather that was slightly torn at the edges. But when she flipped the old, yellowed pages, she was disappointed to find that they were blank.

'What's inside?' asked Arjun from the baluster at the top of the stairs.

'Just an empty book. Wait, there's something on the first page. The writing is a little faint, but I think I can read it.' And saying this, she started to read the words out loud.

'You have opened the book of guile,
May your life be full of bile.
Be a part of your very own ditty,
At the end, trapped for eternity.'

'It doesn't sound ...' But Arjun couldn't complete his sentence as a grey tornado erupted from the pages and caught hold of Anindita. It wrapped itself around her completely, twisting and turning violently. And before anyone could realize what was happening, she had been sucked inside the book.

Arjun couldn't believe his eyes. One moment, his sister had been standing in front of him. The very next, she had disappeared. He stared at the book, lying innocently on the floor. A wisp of black smoke was coming out from its sides. Arjun picked up the book and opened it with trembling fingers. The following words had appeared on the second page: 'Once upon a time, there lived a girl named Anindita. She had ...'

Arjun gulped. It seemed like his sister had been trapped inside the book, and an invisible hand was writing a story about her. He had to get her out. But how? There wasn't any time to think. He would have to find Shwetvardhan.

'Dadi, Anindita and I are going out for a little stroll,' Arjun shouted, sliding the miniature car inside his pocket. And he dashed out before Dadi could ask any questions.

Minutes later, Arjun was travelling across the skies to Jaduprastha. But the journey seemed longer than usual. He kept glancing at the book worriedly. The story had already reached page three.

'Car, please go faster,' he pleaded. 'Anindita's in big trouble.' The car honked and picked up speed. They had soon landed next to the Jaduprastha police station.

Arjun rushed in. 'Anindita's trapped inside,' he cried, waving the book at Dandagupt, the chief of police. 'I need to speak to Shwetvardhan immediately.'

'Oh no, it's the Makkara. Let's go.' The police chief almost dragged Arjun out of the station.

Suvarna Minar was a magnificent circular tower that disappeared into the clouds. It was smooth and golden and towered above everything else. As they approached, a door opened magically. 'It can sense me,' replied Dandagupt, noticing the surprised look on his companion's face. They stepped into the clear glass elevator. 'Gol Kaksh.'

Arjun and Dandagupt barged inside the ornate round chamber where the Mahanagri Parishad had assembled. 'We're sorry to burst in like this,' said the police chief, bowing repeatedly to the astonished elders, 'but this can't wait. Anindita's trapped in the Makkara.'

'How did this happen?' Shwetvardhan ran over and took the book from Arjun. The invisible hand continued to write Anindita's story. 'Tell me everything, but in short.'

Arjun quickly narrated the events of the morning. 'Please get her out,' he pleaded, tearing up.

'I really wish I could. But I'm truly helpless. The spell is irreversible.'

'This can't be happening. I can't go home without Anindita. Who sent her this book?'

But before Shwetvardhan could answer, Pavitranandan spoke up. 'We can deal with that matter later,' he said. 'I think we should be devoting our energies to figuring out how to rescue your sister. And the first thing you should do is meet Chandrakanta. She's a descendent of Dveshakanta.'

'But why will a jadugarni from the dark side help us?' asked Dandagupt.

'She just happens to have a dark lineage. But she doesn't possess any of the malicious traits of her ancestors. Besides, I did her a favour once. I shall inform her that you're on your way.'

Shwetvardhan placed an arm around Arjun. 'Don't worry. I shall accompany you. We shall find a way to get Anindita out of this wretched book.'

'Chandrakanta lives in Bhavya Gadh, which lies in Paschimi Ilaka beyond the northern tip of Kathorikripa. The place is not very far from the vetalas. However, you don't have to worry about them as they keep a safe distance from her.'

Shwetvardhan suggested they take a flying carpet instead of the enchanted car, since it was faster. The luxurious carpet was purple in colour, with a delicate floral pattern woven in gold. It moved like a wave, shaking the golden tassels on its tips eagerly. 'Now hold on tight, because we're in for a really bumpy ride,' said the senior elder, mounting the impatient carpet.

Moments later, they had shot out of Suvarna Minar, with Arjun barely hanging on to an edge with one hand while somehow holding the Makkara close to his chest with the other.

'So what's going on?' shouted Arjun, as the wind rushed against his face. They were miles up in the air, tearing through the bed of clouds towards Paschimi Ilaka.

'Keechad stole the Makkara last night,' replied Shwetvardhan, keeping his eyes peeled as the landscape unfolded below. 'But that's all we really know.'

Arjun squared his jaw. 'I'm going to get that pishacha once all this is over,' he hissed.

'Keechad may be the one directly responsible for the theft, but he's simply a pawn. There are dark forces that are operating from the shadows, and I'm afraid that Chamatkar Nagri is in grave danger. However, for the time being, let's focus our energies on rescuing Anindita from the Makkara. And if I'm not mistaken, that structure looming ahead should be Bhavya Gadh.

Up ahead, a large fort stood on the slopes of a lofty mountain. The fort was surrounded by exotic gardens with ornate fountains.

'This doesn't at all look like the Paschimi Ilaka I remember,' said Arjun, as they descended upon the fort grounds.

A svelte figure dressed in dark purple robes approached them. It was Jadugarni Chandrakanta. Unlike everyone they had encountered from the other side, she was extremely beautiful and radiated an aura of warmth and kindness.

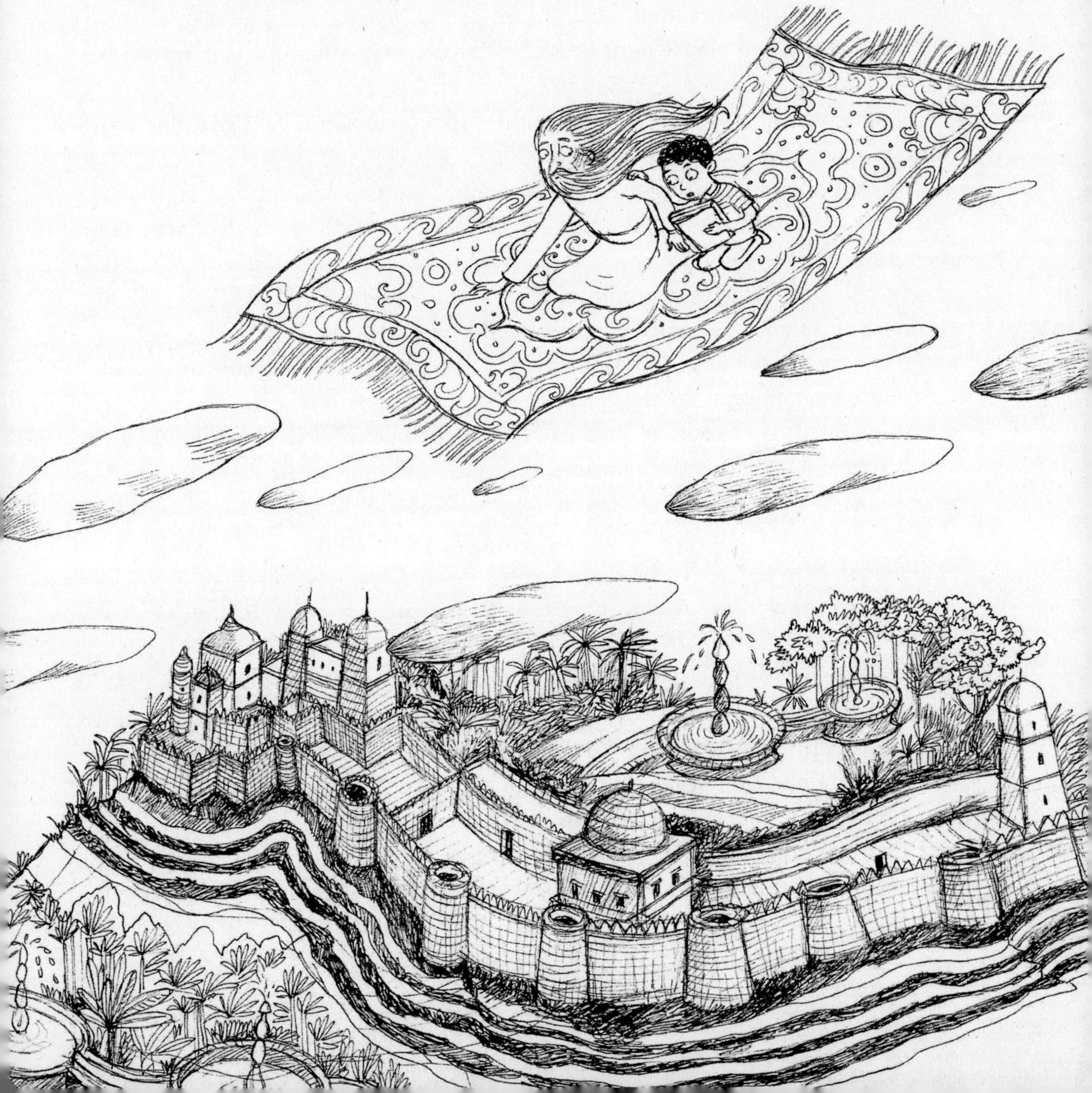

'I've been expecting you,' she said, taking them to a vine-covered pergola nearby. 'Sundari, please lay out the food for our esteemed guests.'

Arjun and Shwetvardan sat down on wooden chairs under the pergola as a ginger-coloured cat placed a tray of delicious-looking food before them.

Chandrakanta looked at them gravely. 'Pavitranandan has already informed me about what has transpired. The burden of Dveshakanta's actions continues to fall upon her descendants.'

'So ... so can you please help Anindita?' asked Arjun anxiously, handing her the Makkara.

Chandrakanta opened the book and flipped ahead. The story had now reached page 20.

'Is there any way to reverse the spell?' asked Shwetvardhan in a worried voice.

'I'm afraid not,' replied Chandrakanta, closing the book with a sigh. She then pointed to a small mark on the top right corner of the cover that looked like an inverted triangle. 'Do you see this? It's faded over time, but it's actually the head of a snake. It means that the spell is irreversible.'

Arjun could feel a tight knot forming at the bottom of his stomach.

'There may be another way though. The spell is definitely irreversible. But that only means that another spell can't be used to counter it. However, I know something about this book that no one else does – as long as the story continues, your sister is still not trapped inside forever. You can think of Anindita being stranded somewhere between the book and our world. But once the story ends, nobody can help her.'

'So how much time do we have?' asked Arjun, his voice brimming with hope. All was not lost just yet.

The jadugarni opened the Makkara again. 'We're on page 20 right now,' she said thoughtfully. 'And this book has 60 pages in all. According to my calculations, it will take a couple of hours to write the rest of her story. So that's how long you have to get her out.'

'What should we do?' asked Shwetvardhan.

'It's quite simple, actually. All you have to do is change the ending of the story. However, you can't use ordinary ink. It has to be sourced from Rangdev, a yaksha from Mayapura. I would suggest you start immediately.'

Shwetvardhan bowed to the jadugarni. 'We're eternally grateful for all your help.'

'I do hope you can save your sister, Arjun,' said Chandrakanta. She turned to the senior elder. 'There's one more thing I wanted to warn you about. I've heard rumours about a conspiracy being hatched against Chamatkar Nagri. Please keep your eyes and ears open.'

Soon, they were airborne, on their way to meet the yaksha who made magical inks. Meanwhile, Anindita's story had already reached page 23.

Mayapura was a quaint land nestled between Khilonapatnam, Mithaspur, Jaduprastha and Tashkot. Shops selling cheap magical wares lined its narrow, cobbled lanes. The shopkeepers' assistants stood outside, yelling at the top of their voices to attract passersby.

'Spices from Guptvan! Breathe out fire like a chakora! Only two gold mudras!'

'This wooden parrot can tell your fortune – only five pieces left!'

'Drink this special tea to grow two inches taller – two for the price of one!'

It was the kind of place Arjun would have loved to explore. However, time was running out, and they had to find Rangdev.

'There,' said Shwetvardhan, pointing to a secluded corner of Mayapura.

The dimly lit shop was built from thick logs of wood. Large, black cauldrons that gave off strange fumes stood in the back. The walls were covered with hundreds of meticulously labelled bottles and assorted ingredients that were used to create magical inks. A slender yaksha with sharp features sat at the counter, making entries in a large ledger. It was Rangdev, dressed in a hat and tunic that had once been white but was now covered in black blotches. 'How may I help you?' he asked, looking up from the top of his thin gold-rimmed glasses.

'We need a special ink that can be used to write in the Makkara,' said Shwetvardhan, placing the book in front of him. 'It's very urgent.'

The yaksha picked up the book and ran his nose around the edges. 'I've heard of this book,' he said, opening it. He felt the texture of the paper before smelling it again and finally taking a lick for good measure. 'This paper is very old and carries a lot of enchantments – dark enchantments. I don't have the ink ready, but I should be able to make some in about 20 minutes.'

Arjun gulped. Another 20 minutes. The story had already reached page 31. But there wasn't any other option. 'Please complete it as soon as possible,' he pleaded.

Rangdev went to the back and began his work. He poured some dark liquids into a beaker. He pulled jars from the shelves and emptied their contents. He chanted while waving his hands above the bubbling concoction. It was like watching an artist in action. After about 15 minutes, the yaksha ink-maker finally emerged.

'Is it ready?' asked Arjun, jumping up from the small stool. He had spent the entire time tapping his foot nervously.

But Rangdev shook his head. 'I'm afraid I'm short of one ingredient,' he said sombrely. 'I need a few scales from the skin of a seven-headed serpent. It's the only thing that can make the ink potent enough to write in the Makkara.'

Arjun's shoulders slumped. 'Where in the world are we going to get that?' he cried in despair.

'From the danavas, if I'm not mistaken,' replied Shwetvardhan. 'And fortunately, they happen to be our friends.'

'I hope they're nearby,' said Arjun, glancing worriedly at the book. The story had progressed to page 38.

'They live in the flying city of Vishalwada. The only way to reach them is by using a vimana.'

'A vimana? What's that?'

Shwetvardhan pulled out a small artefact from his long robes. 'This,' he said, holding it between his thumb and index finger. 'I always keep it with me in case I need to visit them for any reason. It's the only vehicle allowed in Vishalwada. I would also suggest you leave the book here.'

A few minutes later, Arjun and Shwetvardhan were travelling upwards in a

conical contraption with small circular windows. The senior elder had found a clearing and enlarged the vimana much to the amazement of his companion. 'It's powered by ether,' he said.

The journey to the city of the danavas went without a glitch, although it did take almost half an hour. Arjun estimated that the story would have progressed by another 10 pages, which would leave only 12 more pages before Anindita was trapped in the Makkara forever.

The vimana rose above the clouds, giving them a spectacular view of an enormous piece of floating rock that was being pummelled by strong air currents from all directions. They had reached Vishalwada.

'Did I mention that the danavas are giants?' said Shwetvardhan, pushing hard to remain upright in the face of the vicious winds.

Arjun was speechless at the sight of the tall, bearded creatures dressed in coarse jute tunics ambling about the hilly terrain. In fact, everything around them was gigantic. They could barely see above the blades of grass, and the pebbles were as large as boulders. Even the butterflies seemed intimidating.

'Taraka,' shouted Shwetvardhan, cupping his hands around his mouth. 'Down here.'

The curly-haired giant, who had been herding sheep, turned around in surprise. 'Shwetvardhan, my dear friend,' he boomed, picking up the senior elder. He placed him on his palm, shielding him from the wind. 'What brings you to Vishalwada?'

'We are in urgent need of the scales of a seven-headed serpent,' replied Shwetvardhan.

'I'm really sorry, my friend, but the seven-headed serpents have gone into hibernation. And we don't have any left in storage either.'

Arjun turned his face to the skies. What could they do now? He was about to turn his head away when his eyes fell upon something shining brightly around Taraka's neck. It was a horn adorned with scales. He quickly pointed it out to Shwetvardhan, who nodded back with a smile.

Arjun jumped out of the vimana even before it had landed properly in Mayapura and rushed to Rangdev's shop. 'I hope this will work,' he said, handing Taraka's horn—now magically shruken—to the yaksha.

Rangdev held it against the light and nodded.

As he went inside, Arjun opened the Makkara. But a horrible surprise awaited him. The story had already reached page 59. His calculations had been off. 'Please hurry,' he shouted frantically. 'It's almost reached the last page.'

The yaksha master came running out with a bowl. It was filled with a black liquid that swished around violently, giving off a golden tinge. He handed Arjun a quill just as Shwetvardhan reached there.

'What should I write?' asked Arjun, his hand trembling with fear.

'Write clearly that you want Anindita back,' replied the senior elder. 'Quickly. The story's almost over.'

Arjun dipped the quill in the turbulent ink and wrote on the last page:

Anindita returned to Mayapura safely.

The pages of the Makkara flapped rapidly, and the book slammed shut with a loud wail, throwing out a grey tornado once again. When the dust cleared, they could see Anindita standing in front of them. Arjun ran forward and hugged his sobbing sister tightly.

'It was so scary,' wept Anindita. 'I was trapped inside this dark room with two windows. I could see everything happening in this world through one window. But the other window opened into a place filled with frightening creatures. And every time a page turned, I moved farther away from you and closer to this ... this ...'

Shwetvardhan held her close. 'Don't worry, child, you're safe now,' he said, nodding gratefully at the yakhsha. He removed the crystal ball from his robes and chanted a few words. 'Bodhidharma, we've rescued Anindita. But I'm afraid a dark shadow looms upon Chamatkar Nagri.'

'Are you sure?' asked Bodhidharma, deep lines clouding his tall brow. 'We haven't been able to detect any conspiracy yet.'

'I'm quite certain. Our enemies are aware of the role Arjun and Anindita have played in thwarting their plans against our land. Sending the Makkara to Anindita was a ploy to trap her, so as to prevent them from helping us. While this part of their plan hasn't worked, they have succeeded in distracting us.'

'What do you propose we do?'

'I shall be returning to Suvarna Minar. Meanwhile, please be extremely vigilant.'

'And what about us?' asked Anindita

'It is best you return to Manav Lok immediately.'

Arjun nodded, pressing the bridge of his nose. 'I agree,' he sighed. 'If we don't reach home soon, Dadi will be worried. And besides, I think you need some rest as well.'

After thanking Shwetvardhan, Arjun and Anindita went home in their enchanted car. But they were too tired to notice that the sky had taken on grainy hues of pale orange.

KROORADASA'S REVENGE

'Shwetvardhan, the sky has changed colour,' said Bodhidharma grimly, as he entered Gol Kaksh at the very top of Suvarna Minar.

'I'm well aware,' sighed Shwetvardhan, emerging out of the clouds that had wafted inside.

Bodhidharma watched as a few wisps of orange floated by. 'You know what this means, right?' he said, glancing up. 'Although I can't understand how this could have happened. You don't think the kalpanic pranis have anything to do with this, do you?'

'I doubt that. But I knew something was wrong the moment I heard that Keechad had stolen the Makkara. While we were distracted with events related to its theft, our enemies have greatly benefited.'

'What do you mean?' asked Pavitranandan.

'Do you realize today is Ghor Amavasya? A lunar eclipse with all the moons aligned perfectly occurs only once in a thousand years. Our enemies have made use of this time to awaken a great evil. I'm afraid we may not be able to save Chamatkar Nagri this time.'

'But how is this possible? I thought the curse could only be broken if the kalpanic pranis used the Key of Avatar to unlock the gateways to Manav Lok.'

'I confess that's what we assumed all along. But usually, when it comes to such matters, the more pertinent question is whether it's possible to gain access to the magic that can make it happen. Our enemies have obviously used this period to source some very powerful dark enchantments from a bygone era. We could have taken steps to prevent this had we known their intentions, but it's too late now.'

Bodhidharma leaned forward. 'So what can we do?' he asked in a worried voice.

'While we can't undo what's already been set in motion, we must commence work on spells to protect us against the forces of evil. We should also send out messages to all our friends, seeking their support. Although we might fall short even then.'

'What if we use the spell created by Raja Vayumitra and the Mahanagri Parishad a century ago?'

'That was the first thing that came to my mind as well. But, so far, our enemies have been a few steps ahead of us. I'm quite sure they would have taken measures to counter our actions.'

'Do you have any idea who might be behind all this?' asked Gyandarshan, furiously flipping through the pages of a book of enchantments.

'Chamatkar Nagri has many powerful foes. It could be any of them. But I have a feeling that this time, we're not up against just one dark power.'

Pavitranandan walked over to the window. 'We still have a good four hours or so before the sun sets,' he said, his voice laced with hope.

'I'm not sure it will suffice. Nevertheless, we shan't go down meekly. Please start contacting all the kings immediately. Send messages to all our friends, including the chakoras, kalpanic pranis and the danavas. We will need all the help we can get.'

As the elders moved out, Shwetvardhan noticed a piece of cloud that had settled upon his robes. It was already a shade darker.

Meanwhile, in Manav Lok ...

Arjun and Anindita had returned from Chamatkar Nagri shaken and exhausted. They found a note on the table saying Dada and Dadi had gone out to visit some friends and would be late.

They quickly ate the lunch Dadi had kept out and went upstairs to their room. Anindita fell asleep almost immediately. Arjun, however, couldn't get Shwetvardhan's words out of his mind. Could the Makkara have been a diversionary tactic? Could someone be actually plotting against Chamatkar Nagri? He kept tossing and turning, but the thoughts just wouldn't go away.

After an hour, Arjun finally kicked away his blanket and got out of bed. *Perhaps I should contact Shwetvardhan*, he thought. But how? Why hadn't they just stayed back? Arjun shook his head and dragged himself to the basin for a quick wash. He splashed cold water on his face and looked into the mirror. But instead of his own reflection, he found the senior elder's face staring back at him.

'Arjun, we really need your help,' said Shwetvardhan in a grave voice. 'You've got us out of some very difficult situations in the past. But this time, it's serious. I would understand if you don't want to come after everything you've been through. So all I can do is make a request. If things get out of hand, I promise to return you to Manav Lok immediately.'

'I'll leave for Jaduprastha right away. We'll definitely find a way to solve whatever problem it is. But I think Anindita should stay back after all that's happened.'

'I'm sending the door to bring you to Suvarna Minar. It's not safe for you to travel by the enchanted car at this time. I'll explain everything later.'

Arjun quickly wiped his face and ran out. The door had already appeared in their room. But just as he was about to twist the knob, he heard a loud yawn from the bed.

'Why ... why is there a door in the room?' asked Anindita groggily. She yawned again and turned around. But before she could fall asleep again, her mind registered what was happening and her eyes popped open. 'Wait, that's the door to Chamatkar Nagri, isn't it? What's it doing here?'

'Shwetvardhan has sent it for me,' replied Arjun reluctantly. 'I think Chamatkar Nagri's in trouble.'

Anindita sat up with a start. 'You're not going anywhere without me,' she insisted.

'It's going to be very dangerous, Anindita. And besides, you've been through a lot since morning. I think you should get some rest.'

'I don't care. I'm coming with you.'

Arjun decided it would just be easier to say yes and save them some time.

'Wait, don't forget your backpack. It may be useful.'

Moments later, they were standing in Gol Kaksh in the presence of the elders of the Mahanagri Parishad.

'They're hard to miss, aren't they?' sighed Shwetvardhan, pointing to the orange clouds hovering in the room. 'As you can see, the skies have turned a grainy orange. It means that the parnalas are returning to life.'

'But I distinctly recall you saying that only the Key of Avatar could do that,' said Arjun. 'And as we already know, it doesn't exist. So how is this possible?'

'Perhaps you should explain everything from the beginning, Shwetvardhan,' said Bodhidharma. 'Some of the younger elders are not familiar with the details.'

The senior elder sat at the helm of the table with a tired nod. 'The parnalas were the guardians of Chamatkar Nagri for thousands of years. Due to an ancient curse, they were stone statues by day and came to life only at night. However, during the reign of Raja Sherdil, an evil jadugar by the name of Gundasana had promised to grant them eternal life if they helped him conquer Chamatkar Nagri. The unholy alliance was defeated, but they kept launching attacks against Chamatkar Nagri and Kalpanadweep—who had sided with us in the battle—from beyond the mountains in the southeast. It was around this time that Raja Avatar created the key to help the kalpanic pranis escape to Manav Lok. Then, about a century ago, as you already know, Raja Vayumitra and the Mahanagri Parishad brought an end to the parnala menace by turning them to stone permanently. It's been assumed ever since that the only way they could be restored to life was if the kalpanic pranis used the Key of Avatar to open the gateways to Manav Lok.'

'So what's bringing them to life now?' asked Anindita.

'While we don't know exactly how, we have received news that some jadugars from Paschimi Ilaka are responsible. The sky has already turned a dark orange. When it turns brown, the process will be complete.'

Arjun turned his gaze to the vast, blazing firmament. 'So how long do we have?'

'About two hours.'

'What if we attack them right now, when they are still statues? If we don't allow them to come to life, Chamatkar Nagri could be saved.'

Bodhidharma wrung his hands in despair. 'That would have been a great option had we had some time to prepare,' he replied. 'Besides, the jadugars of Paschimi Ilaka would have no doubt taken adequate precautions to ensure that the parnalas are protected until they return to life. We also don't know what other dark enchantments they've got their hands on.'

Just then, Gyandarshan walked in with a solemn expression. 'I'm afraid there's more bad news,' he sighed. 'Our spies have just sent confirmed reports that Krooradasa is behind the entire conspiracy. And he's been joined by Dushtasura, Ghrunadasi, the vetalas and other enemies of Chamatkar Nagri. They've managed to put aside their own differences in their zeal to destroy our land.'

Everyone fell silent. The thought of such formidable foes coming together was a very scary one indeed.

'What will be their first target?' asked Arjun.

'Suvarna Minar,' replied Shwetvardhan. 'If they succeed, taking over the rest of Chamatkar Nagri will be easy.'

'Does the enemy have any weaknesses?'

'They all have individual weaknesses, but collectively, they are very powerful. They've also had the advantage of planning this campaign meticulously, while we're operating in defence. So they've probably factored in every possible counter-measure we can come up with.'

Arjun chewed on the tip of his thumb. The enemy seemed to have done all its homework. Things were looking quite bleak. Were Chamatkar Nagri's days numbered?

'We've asked the kings of Chamatkar Nagri and our friends to be ready as well. They've all begun to take positions around Jaduprastha.'

Arjun dug his chin into his right shoulder. 'While I agree that we're not in a position to attack, I'm just not convinced about the way we're approaching this,' he sighed. 'If we become too defensive against a stronger enemy, they will easily overpower us. What about the parnalas? Is there any way we can single them out?'

'Unfortunately, their bodies are so hard, most of the enchantments simply bounce off,' replied Pavitranandan. 'And while we've recreated the spell used by Raja Vayumitra and the Mahanagri Parishad to turn them to stone, it's the first thing Krooradasa would have thought of as well.'

'Then we need to buy some more time,' said Arjun thoughtfully. 'So while we can't attack, we can certainly create spells that will focus on slowing them down. While this is a defensive strategy, it's still better than simply waiting for them to attack and then trying to counter their spells.'

There were quick nods of approval from around the table.

'Then it's decided,' said Bodhidharma, the urgency evident in his voice as a cloud with deep red hues entered Gol Kaksh.

As the elders got busy working on the spells, Anindita turned to her brother.

'Do you think you can find a way to defeat Krooradasa and the others?'

Arjun pushed his hands behind his head and leaned back. 'It's not looking good at all,' he said. 'We hardly have any time to come up with a strategy. And frankly, even if we had the time, I'm not sure we can defeat this enemy. Together, they are just too powerful.'

Anindita slumped back in her chair, and Arjun returned to his thoughts.

Almost an hour later, Shwetvardhan returned. 'The spells are ready,' he said. 'Do you have any other suggestions?'

'The parnalas will launch an attack from the air, right?' asked Arjun.

The senior elder nodded.

'Then we should have our forces ready to fight them in the air. But somehow, I fear it will only delay the inevitable.'

Shwetvardhan patted Arjun's back. 'It's okay,' he said sadly. 'You've done enough for us. There's nothing more you can do. It's better I send you back before the parnalas get here.'

Before Arjun could react, Gyandarshan came running up. 'Someone's approaching us.'

The elders and the children rushed to the window. They could see two hideous creatures flying at them through the brown skies. The parnalas had risen once again after a hundred years. They were winged creatures with a large horn rising out of their uncharacteristically small heads and sharp fangs jutting out of their bulbous lips. They moved through the air like serpents, their tails swimming behind them, just as Shwetvardhan had described.

'We come in peace, for now,' boomed a loud voice. 'Accept our demands, and no one shall get hurt.'

As the parnalas emerged out of the curdled clouds, the familiar figures of Krooradasa and Keechad also became visible.

Shwetvardhan held up his hand, indicating that no one should use any magic. The withered frame of the evil jadugar appeared, proudly perched atop his massive parnala. 'I'm sure you've met Paatki, King of the Parnalas,' he snickered, 'the very same ones your Mahanagri Parishad turned to stone.'

The senior elder folded his hands quietly. 'I thought you came here with an offer.'

Krooradasa's yellow eyes glowered wickedly. 'Come, come, Shwetvardhan, what's the hurry?' he asked, his voice dripping with venom. He suddenly noticed the two children. 'I see you've brought the pests from Manav Lok as well. That's perfect. Ghrunadasi would love to get her hands on them as would a lot of my friends.'

'If you have a proposal to share, please do so now or leave.'

The evil jadugar's emaciated body trembled with rage. 'How dare you use that tone with me?' he screamed. 'You very well know that I can destroy this puny tower right now. Keechad, tell them our demands.'

A second parnala flew forward with the bald pishacha mounted uncomfortably upon its large back.

'We have three demands,' he shouted, his protruding eyes fixed on them menacingly. 'First, the Mahanagri Parishad should hand over Suvarna Minar to us and cross over into Patala, never to return. Second, all the creatures of Chamatkar Nagri should become our slaves and serve us faithfully. Third, Raja Balushahi should become Jadugar Krooradasa's personal assistant.'

'And our last demand is that the two meddlesome children of Manav Lok should be handed over to us,' added the evil jadugar, glaring at them. 'You have 15 minutes to deliberate on our proposition. If you agree, I give you my personal assurance that no creature of Chamatkar Nagri shall be harmed.'

'The answer is no,' replied Shwetvardhan in a quiet voice. 'You don't have to wait another minute.'

'You shall all pay dearly for your impudence,' screamed Krooradasa, as the parnalas turned around and disappeared into the muddy haze.

'The forces of Krooradasa have already breached our outermost enchantments,' said Pavitranandan. 'If they continue at this rate, they shall reach Suvarna Minar in another 15 minutes. What should we do?'

'We've done all that we could do,' replied Shwetvardhan, staring into the brown void that was lighting up from time to time with blue flashes. He slowly turned around with a weary look. 'I'm afraid I don't see a way out of this predicament. It's time to send the children back. They've done much more than was expected of them. We can't ask for anything else.'

'I'm not ready to give up yet,' said Arjun determinedly. 'There has to be a solution. But I think Anindita should go back.'

'As if that's going to happen,' retorted Anindita. 'We'll find a way together.'

'You are true allies of Chamatkar Nagri,' said Shwetvardhan. 'But you really must leave now. Once the parnalas attack, I may not be able to send you to Manav Lok.'

Suddenly, Bodhidharma's voice rang through Gol Kaksh. 'We have only five minutes before the enemy reaches Suvarna Minar.'

As everyone ran to the windows, they could see thousands upon thousands of jadugars from Paschimi Ilaka sitting astride the vicious parnalas, hurling flashes of blue at the final layer of enchantments that had been cast around Jaduprastha by the elders. And as the attacks intensified, cracks slowly began to appear in the protective shield.

'All elders, assume your positions now,' said Shwetvardhan, raising his wand. 'Gyandarshan, intimate all the kings of Chamatkar Nagri and all our friends to be ready to defend the tower.'

'Arjun, do you think we should take the enchanted car and help out?' whispered Anindita, tugging at his sleeve.

Arjun was about to shake his head when he stopped and stared at his red backpack, which was lying in a corner. He tapped his knuckles against his teeth a few times, deep in thought. Suddenly, he ran over and unzipped the backpack, emptying out its contents hastily. There was a loud clang as a gleaming object spilled upon the floor. He picked it up with a sigh of relief. 'I've got it,' he shouted. 'We can defeat Krooradasa without a war.'

The elders, who had been watching the collapse of the protective shield with growing apprehension, turned around expectantly.

'We need to hurry,' said Shwetvardhan, taking a few steps back, his wand still drawn.

Arjun handed Aladdin's lamp to Anindita with a nod. She quickly rubbed it.

Abu, the lamp's jinn, appeared in a burst of golden smoke.

'What is your wish, my mistress?' he asked, bowing deeply.

'Please turn all the parnalas to stone,' said Anindita immediately.

Everyone expected the dark brown creatures to fall from the skies to their doom. But alas, it wasn't to be.

'I'm sorry, my mistress,' said Abu regretfully. 'But a wish that intends to cause harm to another living being cannot be granted according to the rules of Jinntara. And since you were aware of this, you have lost the wish.'

Saying this, the jinn disappeared back into the lamp.

A gloomy hush descended upon the room at this sudden turn of events. Outside, the forces of Krooradasa had almost broken through. But Arjun remained composed. 'We do have one more wish,' he said, turning to face his sister. 'And this is what I want you to say.'

Anindita listened closely and then rubbed the lamp once again.

'What is your wish, my mistress?' asked Abu, materializing before them once again.

'My wish is that Chamatkar Nagri and its friends should always be protected from their enemies,' replied Anindita, measuring each word carefully.

'Your wish is my command.'

Peace had returned to Chamatkar Nagri. The enemy had breached the final defences cast by the elders and charged towards Suvarna Minar, only to realize that their wands had become powerless. The battle had been lost even before it had begun. Moments later, Jaduprastha was witness to a mass exodus of the forces of Krooradasa. And in the confusion that reigned, the once tightly knit alliance broke apart, with the various factions hurling abuses at the evil jadugar responsible for the fiasco.

Krooradasa and Ghrunadasi were chased into Patala by the vetalas. And Keechad, having slipped off his mount as they were fleeing Jaduprastha, once again landed in prison, much to Arjun's delight. With the enemy vanquished, the elders turned the parnalas to stone again.

The kings of Chamatkar Nagri soon joined Arjun and Anindita and the elders in Gol Kaksh.

'This is the closest our land has come to being destroyed since the Mahayudh nearly three centuries ago,' said Shwetvardhan, glancing contentedly at the indigo skies outside. 'I really thought that even a miracle couldn't save us today. Chamatkar Nagri shall always remain indebted to the two of you.'

The children blushed at this effusive praise from the senior elder even as the others gave them a round of applause.

'Arjun and Anindita,' said Shwetvardhan, waving his wand and conjuring up two golden stars, 'by the power vested in me, I now bestow upon you these Suvarna Taras, the highest medals of honour that can be awarded in Chamatkar Nagri. We only award one each century, but I'm sure everyone will agree that an exception is justified this time around. These are not being given to you for saving the land but because you chose to be with us in our time of need. You deserve them.'

'I'm so glad we didn't use the remaining wishes,' whispered Anindita, squeezing her brother's hand. He nodded back excitedly, staring at the shiny golden medals hanging around their necks.

The elders and the kings stepped forward and gave them both tight hugs.

'I'm sure you must be tired,' said Shwetvardhan. 'But this is one occasion when we won't let you go anywhere. Because it's time for a celebration, the likes of which even Chamatkar Nagri has never seen before.'

And as Arjun and Anindita get ready to have the time of their lives, let us bid them goodbye. Here's wishing them many more marvellous adventures to come.

AUTHOR

Prashant Pinge loves stringing words together to create enchanting stories for children. He also utterly disregards reality. Little wonder then that he prefers to reside in 16th-century England next to the Bard's house, and spend his days in the company of his characters and nights taming dragons. He does surface from time to time, though, to update his website http://prashantpinge.com

ILLUSTRATOR

Priya Kuriyan is a children's book illustrator, comic-book artist and an animator. A graduate of the National Institute of Design (Ahmedabad), she has directed educational films for the Sesame Street Show (India) and the Children's Film Society of India (CFSI), and illustrated numerous children's books for various Indian publishers. She currently lives in Bangalore, filling her sketchbooks with strange caricatures of its residents. You can see her work at http://priyakurian.blogspot.com